TREES. TREES WERE THE PROBLEM.

Angela Jordan knew, since the age of five, that she had a unique gift. A gift that wasn't her witchy magic. A gift she wouldn't exactly call a "gift."

The demon hunter who'd rescued her that first time in the church parking lot, Aidan, called it a gift. Angie thought her ancestors had done something millennia ago to piss off a druid and all these centuries later, she got stuck with the curse.

Trees. Trees were the problem.

And at that moment, she was surrounding by them.

HOWLING DREADFUL ON A MOONLIT STRANGE

A DEMON WITCH PREQUEL DUOLOGY

KAT SIMONS

T&D PUBLISHING

Howling Dreadful

on a

Moonlit Strange

KAT SIMONS

AUTHOR OF THE CARY REDMOND SERIES

Howling Dreadful

A DEMON WITCH STORY

Howling Dreadful

CHAPTER ONE

$\mathcal{A}$ngela Jordan knew, since the age of five, that she had a unique gift. A gift that wasn't her witchy magic. A gift she wouldn't exactly call a "gift."

The demon hunter who'd rescued her that first time in the church parking lot, Aidan, called it a gift. Angie thought her ancestors had done something millennia ago to piss off a druid and all these centuries later, she got stuck with the curse.

Trees. Trees were the problem.

And at that moment, she was surrounding by them.

On purpose. Because Aidan had asked.

She was not a happy woman right now.

"I am not a happy woman right now," she muttered.

"So you've said," Aidan said quietly. "A few times."

A small snort from Aidan's protégé, Sebastian, didn't help.

Angie was trying very hard not to think too much about the demon hunter's protégé.

Sebastian was… Well, he should have been one of the most ordinary people she'd ever seen. Aidan was. Aidan had ordinary brown hair, currently pulled into an ordinary braid. She had an ordinary build. Was an ordinary average height. Had an ordinary pale complexion with no distinguishing facial marks like freckles or moles. Had an ordinary average face. She wasn't too attractive or too unattractive to draw attention. She wasn't too tall or too short. Her ordinary brown hair brushed her shoulders, when it was loose, always in a non-descript hairstyle. She didn't have any obvious scars, tics, disabilities, or extraordinary attributes. She didn't dress to stand out in a crowd. She didn't draw attention to herself in any way.

The demon hunter was as unremarkable, as easy to overlook, as any person Angie had ever met.

Until, of course, you looked into her eyes.

And really, unless you knew what you were looking at, it was pretty easy to dismiss that flash of red in the brown depths as a trick of the light.

Sebastian, on the other hand, was *not* easy to overlook. He was as tall as, maybe taller than, Angie's six-foot height, with wide shoulders, a lean, athletic frame, and a ridiculously handsome face. Really ridiculous. Men weren't this handsome in real life. Movie stars were this handsome. Soap stars were this handsome. But not men you met through an old acquaintance.

His dark brown hair was cut short and tight to his head,

his dark brown skin was smooth and ageless, his jaw clean shaven. He was dressed simply enough in a black t-shirt and dark colored jeans, but he filled out the jeans and t-shirt in ways that was impossible to ignore and that did funny, fluttery things to her stomach. He moved with an easy, lethal grace that reminded her of a predator. One of the big lazy ones. One of the cats—a lion or a jaguar. The ones you could fool yourself into thinking were just soft, snuggly animals. Right before they ripped your throat out.

She'd have thought that edge of danger would have her thoroughly on guard with him, not in any way distracted by the subtle spice of his scent. And she would have been wrong.

The red flash in the depths of his dark brown eyes was a little fainter than Aidan's. Easier to dismiss. Easier to pretend it wasn't there. But unlike Aidan, he didn't blend in to his surroundings. He stood out. A beacon call of handsomeness that demanded she look and appreciate and dwell on.

It was infuriating.

She tried not to study him. Tried to keep her attention on the situation at hand—demon had broken loose, they needed her to ensure it went back to a demon realm, lots of dangerous stuff about to happen. But she kept…staring at Sebastian. Getting caught in the way his mouth quirked when he was amused. The way he let his gaze linger on her. The way he moved.

She jerked her gaze away from him. Again.

He was almost as dangerous to look at as the surrounding trees.

"Something funny?" she asked, her tone as brittle as she could make it while her heart was pounding so hard.

"Nothing at all," he said, his voice low.

To add insult to injury, the man had a deep, smoky voice and an English accent that danced like little sparks of fire down her spine. Just…unfair!

"This is a serious situation," she said, her tone harsh because she was embarrassed and disoriented. "One I shouldn't be involved in." This last she directed to Aidan.

"You'll be fine," Aidan said. "You've been working with Esmerelda."

"On my magic," she said. "Not…this."

Well, not *this* in a while. Esmerelda was her first magical mentor, and still one of her most influential. She'd known Esmerelda since she was five years old. After her mother—the only moderately magical person in her immediate family—had approved the pairing. Aidan had brought Esmerelda into her life, something Angie would be forever grateful for.

And so, yes, she did feel like she owed Aidan. Help at least. Since Aidan had helped her. But this wasn't…

She'd have preferred using her ordinary witch magic. The magic she was called to. Spells, harnessing the elements, even her touch psychic skills… Anything but *this*.

"I have midterms next week. I should be studying for those." She was in her senior year at University of New Mexico. She was due to graduate this spring with her Bachelors in Psychology—if she didn't fail her fall classes because she got sucked into helping Aidan with demons.

"What classes? Maybe I can help," Sebastian said.

She tried to ignore the way her toes curled at the sound of his voice. "No." She couldn't imagine trying to study with him around. She couldn't imagine trying to *think* with him too close.

And why was he letting her see him like this? Hmm? He was a *demon hunter*. He could ensure she saw him in any way he wanted, with just his will. It was one of their best tricks, blending in, fading into the background, looking harmless and ordinary. She had no idea if Aidan *really* looked so ordinary. But she knew Sebastian *could* make himself look ordinary and harmless or he wouldn't have been able to do this job for very long. Didn't do to stand out to the humans who summoned demons. They might remember you later. Demon hunters didn't want to be remembered. If someone remembered them, they might think to call a demon and target them. Demon hunters had to be forgettable.

Angie could never easily forget Sebastian.

He had to be doing this on purpose. He had to be. And that was what pissed her off so much.

They moved as quietly through the woods as the crunchy fall undergrowth allowed, which, given they were hunters and she was a witch with ties to the elements, meant they managed it better than the humans in the distance. The men were making enough noise to cover any approach anyway, but demons had better hearing than humans so it was safer to be cautious.

When she finally got a look at the spot in the woods the humans had staked out—so to speak—for their demon summoning, Angie frowned. They'd cleared a space in an open patch of ground, pushing away all the leaf and twig detritus until there was only smooth, dark dirt. And then they'd formed a circle using rocks. A good, sturdy base. As good as chalk and more stable in the dirt than chalk might have been. Obviously, they hadn't planned to let their demon out.

There were candles dotted around the circle, just outside the rocks, illuminated the scene in wobbly orange light and filling the clearing with the waxy scent of candle fire. Angie looked at the dried leaves at the outer edge of the clearing and shook her head. Fire hazard this time of year, having unguarded candles. Even if they'd cleared space for it. Sparks flew off candles, especially during ceremonies when elements like wind could kick up more.

The little flickering flames danced in a gentle breeze, as if in answer to her thought. But so far, no sparks had jumped. One less thing to worry about immediately.

Despite Aidan's warning, though, it was obvious the demon hadn't escaped the circle yet. It was still firmly inside the stones as the three human men who'd summoned it danced around the circle, making whooping noises and chanting something Angie couldn't make out. Most of her focus was on the demon.

She hadn't seen one like this in... Maybe ever. Not outside their own realms. Except that one time. But never like this. Though technically, being inside the circle linked them to their realms and ensured they weren't fully in the human realm. Even then, she wasn't a hunter so she didn't run around the world stopping idiots who summoned demons, which meant she didn't see these demon summoning ceremonies.

Her history with demons was…different.

This wasn't a demon species she'd encountered before either. Was that good or bad? It was squat and wide and blue-colored, with four leg-like, short, stubby limbs tipped with wickedly long claws. There were tentacles along its back that waved around its blobbish body. Its head was another blob on a blob, though with four glowing red eyes in the center, a set of wicked looking horns curving from its blob head, and a mouth too wide for the round face, filled with an awful lot of sharp teeth.

There was a kind of fog covering the ground inside the circle. Angie couldn't tell if that meant the demon was one of the ones that issued cold rather than heat, or whether it was just part of the summoning.

She hoped it wasn't the cold kind. She couldn't look into those realms, didn't risk it. And if a cold bastard got out, they'd all freeze instantly before they could do anything to stop it.

Despite her curse-gift, she was not a demon expert. She didn't *want* to be a demon expert. That was a demon hunter's job. And she left it to them. Or at least, she'd tried.

"It hasn't escaped," she murmured to Aidan as they stood just inside the treeline, in the shadows outside the uneven candlelight. There wasn't much of a moon overhead. And they'd turned off their flashlights back a ways so the humans didn't notice them approaching. The deep shadows would keep them hidden from the three men dancing around the circle. But even if the darkness hadn't helped, Aidan could *will* the humans not to see them.

"Actually," Aidan said, her voice trailing off as she stared at the circle.

Angie glanced between the hunter and Sebastian. "Well?" she mouthed to him.

He was frowning, his gaze moving between Aidan and the dancing humans. He ignored her question.

She tried really hard not to huff out her irritation. She must not have succeeded though, because his gaze flashed to her and he smiled, very faintly and lethally.

She forgot what she'd asked.

Damn it. This was no time to be distracted. There was a demon *right there*. And she didn't know what it could do. Aidan looked…intent, which probably wasn't a good sign. The dancing men seemed to be chanting louder. The fog inside the containment circle was swirling. And if this was a cold beast instead of a hot one, they might all freeze if it escaped.

But one smile from the absurdly handsome Sebastian and her brain frizzled.

Because she needed the comfort, she rubbed the little pentagram hanging from the beaded bracelet around her wrist. It was a ward, an…aide that helped bring her back from the brink if she accidentally looked into the naturally formed V of a tree. The bracelet was a gift, from Esmerelda, and it helped a lot to keep her focused and harness her reserves when she got sucked into her *other* gift-curse.

Reminded her she was a witch, not a hunter. Reminder her she was in control.

She didn't feel in control right now. She felt wildly out of her depth. She hated that feeling with a deep and abiding passion.

Control was extremely important for her—controlling her magic, controlling her touch psychic skill so she didn't accidentally read every little thing she touched—and feeling out of balance was dangerous.

She pressed the little silver pentagram between her fingers, hard, letting the metal dig into her skin, reminding her who she was. What she was.

Then she started to murmur a little spell. Nothing that would interfere with Aidan and Sebastian's efforts to banish the demon. Just a little something to…help.

She released the pentagram to form the finger gestures necessary to setting the spell, keeping her gaze on the containment circle, the dancing men, the demon, but her mental focus wasn't on her surroundings. It was on calling forth her real power. Her magic tingled in her blood and rose through her feet as she grounded in the earth. Elements were her domain. Not the demon realms.

Not the demon realms.

A snap from the clearing made her heart beat harder. She got her spell to the trigger point then held it in a waiting pattern. One last word and hand gesture would set it into motion. But she wasn't quite ready for it yet.

Neither Aidan nor Sebastian had moved. They stood as still as the surrounding trees. Still enough that if she wasn't hyper aware of Sebastian next to her, she might be under the illusion they'd left.

That was a demon hunter's power. That was their will.

She searched the clearing for the source of the sound that had almost brought her out of her conjuring. The dark woods beyond the clearing were deeply shadowed. She couldn't afford to look too closely, so she kept her gaze angled toward the ground at the base of the trees, looking for movement in the darkness.

There could be more humans out there. Aidan hadn't told her how many were involved in this. Aidan might not even know. Though Angie had a feeling she did. The hunter always seemed to know more than she said.

What she *had* said to Angie was that a demon had escaped and they wanted her help returning it to a demon realm.

They didn't *need* her help, strictly speaking. Since people with her skill were…well, generationally rare. One every four hundred years, if that. Or so Aidan had told her. The demon hunters couldn't rely on someone like Angie to send back escaped demons. They used their skills, knowledge, and most of all their will to do that. Most of the time.

But a freed demon was always more dangerous. They were fully in this realm at that stage. Not linked to their own. And while they sacrificed power to get here, even a weak demon was a deadly demon.

But that was as much about the situation as she knew.

"You said it was free," Angie murmured very quietly to Aidan. "Is there more than one?"

The words left her mouth as the thought occurred to her. The rightness of the question appalled her.

"There is, isn't there?" she asked.

There was more than one. There had to be. That was why Sebastian was here. That was why they'd called her for help. Aidan could handle a demon on her own or she wouldn't still be alive. Aidan could handle more than one demon on her own or she wouldn't still be alive.

Terror caught Angie's throat.

What had to be happening that Aidan brought backup?

"How many are there?" she whispered, swallowing hard. Her heartbeat pounded like a drum, loud enough she was sure the demon in the circle would hear it. She searched the shadowed ground beyond the containment circle again even as the hairs on the back of her neck prickled.

Neither of the demon hunters answered her question. But they didn't need to. The truth hung in the autumn crisp air.

There were more demons in these woods than two demon hunters alone could handle. Demons that were already free.

She was going to need a bigger spell.

CHAPTER TWO

Candle flames crackled in the dark, cool air, the sound of the men chanting around the stone containment circle fading into the background of Angie's panic. Even the blue, blobby demon seemed less of a worry. Because there were loose demons in the woods around them.

Aidan hadn't confirmed that out loud. Sebastian hadn't either.

They didn't have to. Their silence said everything.

The fact that they'd come to her for help, brought her here at all, should have warned her long before this moment.

She wasn't sure she could have gotten less happy than she'd been earlier, when her biggest worry was being surrounded by trees. She was definitely less happy now.

"What do we do?" she murmured for both Aidan and Sebastian.

Aidan raised a hand for silence, so Angie fell silent but

she pressed the pentagram harder into her fingers. She'd have a pentagram shaped bruise at this rate and didn't really care. A tingling through the little warding charm gave her some comfort. Not a lot. But some.

She should be studying for midterms right now. She should be safe in her own apartment, away from demons and trees and the rotten humans who did this. This was Aidan's job. Sebastian's. She was just a college student.

No. She sucked in a quiet but deep breath. Not *just* a college student. Demons might be out of her depth. But she was a witch, a well-trained witch, learning more every day, with no small amount of power at her command. She wasn't helpless. She wasn't defenseless.

She forced herself to think, to work out what they could do. She had one of the best demon hunters in the world at her side—Aidan was legendary, even among the hunters—and she had her magic. She had no idea what Sebastian could do, how strong his will was. If he was Aidan's protégé, then his skills were formidable. That was good. Angie would take that and hope his will was strong enough to keep him alive.

A demon hunter who's will wasn't stronger than a demon's ended up dead.

The thought of Sebastian ending up dead did strange, tightening things to her stomach. She ignored the sensation as best she could. But the fact that it was there at all…

She forced another deep breath. She had one spell ready and waiting to be triggered. But she needed another few ready. She couldn't hold that many un-triggered. So far, her record in a controlled environment with one of her teachers there to help her, and inside the safety of a protection circle just in case something went wrong, was three.

This was not a controlled environment with a convenient teacher and protection circle.

One more, then. She could hold one more. She ran through her repertoire and decided on the second spell. Yes, that would do. And she'd practiced holding it with another spell before, so she knew she could manage it.

She kept her murmured words quiet and her gestures as subtle as possible while not sacrificing precision. Word and hand gestures had to be exact, perfectly shaped and timed, or a spell could go terribly wrong. There were other ways witches did magic. But this was the way she knew and what worked with her innate powers. This was how she had to cast spells.

She felt Sebastian's gaze on the side of her head. She ignored him because she had to concentrate, but the awareness of him noticing her and what she was doing was… difficult to manage.

When her spell was at the last possible point, when all it needed was a single word and one last finger twist to set it into motion, she carefully set it on the mental shelf with her first spell. Within easy reach. Ready to go off. Balanced so they didn't trigger too soon.

"Will it interfere with what Aidan and I do?" Sebastian asked quietly. "The spell you've just done?"

"No," she whispered back, and then had to clamp her mouth shut to keep from explaining more to him.

First, she didn't want to draw the attention of the still

dancing humans or any of the demons in the woods around them—that last was probably a pointless hope, but still. Second, it wasn't his business how her magic worked. Her witchy skills weren't the reason Aidan had brought her anyway. But she also didn't discuss the specifics with an outsider.

He probably should know, her conscious told her. At least which spells she had ready to trigger. He and Aidan both probably needed to know so they knew what to expect. He didn't need to know *how* she cast, but understanding what she was about to cast was probably important.

She opened her mouth to tell him and Aidan both what she had at the ready, but a noise from the trees silenced her.

Even without Aidan's raised hand, Angie froze.

The ground vibrated beneath her, a tremor like the rumbling after an earthquake. Slight aftershock, but not the big one. Except this was before the earthquake. And the shaking rumble got louder, and more intense, as the moments ticked past.

The dancing men sent up a whooping shout, a cheer. Their voices sounded harsh and scratchy, like they'd been chanting so long they'd nearly ruined their throats.

Across the small clearing, beyond the blue demon and the stone circle, the first flickering of red light came into view, lighting the dark night.

Angie was tempted to look up into the trees, to search the trees for the first glimpse of the approaching demon—or demons—but to do so risked an accidental encounter with just the wrong type of tree. She didn't want to loose *more* demons onto this realm than might already be here.

More glowing red filled the woods beyond the circle. And with a shiver of fear, Angie realized there was red glowing in her peripheral vision, too. She swallowed hard. Keeping her gaze near the ground, she glanced beyond Sebastian, then Aidan.

Fuck. Lots of red glow. Lot of approaching demons.

The hair on the back of her neck prickled. Demons from the rear as well.

It took everything in her not to swing around and face the threat at her back. Being surrounded meant every part of her was vulnerable. Panic robbed her of logic. Again. She had no idea what to do.

Help!

Aidan rested a hand on her arm and very quietly murmured, "Trigger the circle."

Angie didn't even ask how Aidan knew what one of the spells she'd set up was, and she didn't question the hunter's timing. She triggered the second spell she'd designed. The protection circle. Encompassing herself and the two hunters.

A flash of blue light in her witchy vision as the circle closed and a cone of protective energy rose above them. The hunters wouldn't see that blue light. They wouldn't see the circle at all, though Aidan might have felt it go up. But the glow of blue in Angie's mind's eye was the most reassuring thing Angie had ever seen.

She released a slow breath and let her shoulders relax. No demons would get past that. Especially with Aidan and

Sebastian's wills to hold it. They had a little breathing room to work.

"Was that a good idea?" Sebastian murmured—too Aidan, not Angie.

"Yes," Aidan said, her gaze still on the dancing, whooping men.

Angie winced. There was nothing she could do to help the men. At least not at the moment. But since they were actively summoning at least one demon and had filled the woods with more, she wasn't inclined to feel that bad.

Then the first demon came into view. Not one of the giant ones. A small, almost human-sized being with black skin and leathery wings like a bat's, a smoothly bald head, and taloned claws where its fingers and toes would have been. Its eyes were red spots amidst all the blackness. Three more similar demons moved up around the first. All of them so dark, they blended with the shadows, their wings ruffling and red eyes the only thing keeping them visible when they stopped moving.

More demons appeared. More of the small bat-winged creatures. But also some of the larger ones. Some with molten skin, red and rolling like lava over their huge hunched bodies. Others shaped a little like a human and a little like an oxen, moving on two legs but dropping to all fours as they settled into place around the edge of the clearing.

Angie spotted several demons with green scaled skin, their tentacles a white fleshy color that struck her as quite horrible to look at, their bodies shaped like a combination of human tops and octopus bottoms. There were more. Another two of the blue blobby demons, like the one in the circle—which meant they weren't from a froze realm, thank the goddess, or everyone would have frozen by now. A few more with black crackling rock skin over lava. A tentacled, gray-skinned demon walked beside a huge beast that looked like a cross between a bull and an eagle with bright red skin. Almost all of them with glowing red eyes.

The stench of sulfur coated Angie's tongue, making her gag even as she shivered. The last time she'd been around half so many demons, she'd accidentally unleashed them by staring into the natural V in a tree trunk in her father's church parking lot.

And Aidan had to come and put all those demons back.

Angie barely remembered the fight. She was too young and scared, terrified and guilty. Oh so much guilt. For a child, almost too much. Would have been too much if not for Aidan.

Which was why she was here. Surrounded by demons again. Hoping her magical protective circle would keep them safe until Aidan and Sebastian decided what to do.

"So many different kinds," Sebastian murmured. "Idiots."

"The demons or the humans summoning them?" Angie asked, her voice low as she slowly turned.

Behind them three demons stood just outside her circle. Staring in.

Smiling.

The three demons were more of the small, black, bat-winged creatures, with talons for fingers and toes. They made a high, piercing, chittering sound as they stared at Angie, and she stared helplessly back.

No. Not helpless. They couldn't cross her circle. They would have already if they could.

One did test its boundaries, though. Setting the tip of one talon against the cone of light that was only visible in Angie's mind's eye. At least, it was supposed to only be visible that way. The demons seemed to have an exact sense of where the circle began.

The demon's talon sizzled and sparked, and a flash of blue light erupted visibly, making the demon yelp and jump back.

That was helpful.

"Good circle," Aidan murmured. Her gaze was still on the dancing men. She hadn't so much as glanced around at the various species of demons filling in around them.

"Bad situation," Angie whispered back, her throat tight.

"You okay?" Sebastian asked her, leaning a little closer.

"Of course not," she snapped, keeping her voice low still but only because she was too scared to speak any louder. "I'm surrounded by fucking demons."

Sebastian took her hand and squeezed once before releasing her. The touch was so unexpected she didn't know how to react. His hand had been large and warm and… distracting. Distracting enough that she looked away from the demons at their backs to stare at the side of his face.

He didn't turn to look at her.

"Okay," Aidan said, breaking into Angie's confusion. "They're about to release this current demon."

"Why a stone circle if they're letting them out?" Angie muttered. "Why build something that strong and not just use chalk like a normal idiot?"

Sebastian's mouth twitched.

Aidan said, "They're summoning demons from more than one realm. Each realm would need a freshly drawn circle. The stones are more stable for cross-realm summonings and give them control over the release in a way a chalk circle wouldn't.

That was news to Angie—not that she knew much about demons and demon summonings since she tried to avoid all things demon. "I didn't know that about stone circles." She narrowed her eyes, glancing back at the three men. "How did they learn it?"

"Book probably," Aidan said. She gestured to the ground at one side of the stone circle and sure enough there was an open book, the pages fluttering in a wind that had been chilly before the area was surrounded by demons.

"What's their plan? What's the point of all this?" Sebastian whispered, but more like he was talking to himself and not to either his mentor or Angie.

"Motivations don't really matter," Aidan said, answering Sebastian's questions even if they hadn't been meant for her. "It's always the same anyway. Greed, or desperation, or some variation on that theme."

"What do we do?" Angie asked. Again. Because the three demons behind them were still testing her circle. And she could feel the others. All around them. How many? Did the exact number even matter?

"We need to prevent that new one from being released," Aidan said.

"Why didn't you guys get here sooner?" Angie asked, her heart pounding too hard, making spots dance at the edge of her vision. "When there was only one or two demons? How were they allowed to get away with releasing so many? And why aren't the humans dead?"

Aidan, her attention still intent on the dancing men, said, "We'll ask if we can keep them from dying now."

"As to why we weren't here sooner," Sebastian said, "we're here as early as we could get here. This has all happened…fast."

"This doesn't make sense," Angie muttered. "These demons are from different realms. Shouldn't they be killing each other?"

She actually had no idea. For all she knew, demons from different realms might cooperate and not kill each other, as well as everything in sight, if there was a big enough end goal.

She hadn't taken her attention from the bat-winged beasts at their backs, but the demons were just looking at them now. No longer testing her circle. The one who'd been running its talon over her circle's protective barrier had its mouth lifted in what might have been a teeth-filled smile. It was hard to tell if that was a smile or not. But the display of all those sharp sharp teeth was easy enough to interpret.

Aidan made a little move next to Angie, a sort of abrupt intake of air, not quite a gasp and not very obviously a gesture, but it was movement from the otherwise still hunter. The gesture drew Angie's full attention.

"What is it?"

"Almost time," Aidan murmured. Her voice sounded distant now, as if she wasn't actually answering the question but was talking to herself, her concentration elsewhere.

"Sebastian?" Angie asked quietly, leaning a little closer to him without meaning to.

He didn't respond. That wasn't reassuring.

"When they reach the stage of releasing this last demon," Aidan said, quietly, "they'll have to reset to start a new summoning."

"Shouldn't we, you know, prevent them from releasing yet another demon?" Angie's voice didn't squeak when she got nervous, not much or often. But her voice did deepen and she heard the drop in register clearly. Everything in her screamed to get away. She hadn't felt this out of her depth and helpless since that parking lot when she was five.

"There's a plan," Aidan murmured, yet again seeming like she was mostly talking to herself. "The release of so many is part of the bargain they've made. That's why they're not dead."

"Huh?"

"They aren't…" Aidan paused as if listening. "Even free, the demons are still bound by the bargain they've made with the three men. The rules of that bargain allow them out of the circle but not out of the bargain. That's why the humans aren't dead."

Sebastian glanced away from the dancing men, to the

three demons still standing behind them. "What bargain? For what?"

The demon in the middle of the triad opened his mouth again in that teeth-revealing gesture that might have been a smile if its face were even a little bit human-like.

It hissed out a sound that made Angie shiver. A sound that hurt her ears. And it took a full beat before she translated the hiss into words…

"To rule."

CHAPTER THREE

o rule?

The demon's hissed response raised more questions for Angie than it answered. To rule what? To rule whom? This realm? Who would rule? Why like this? Why not a bigger, more powerful demon?

Angie might not know much about demons, on purpose, but she knew enough to know if the demons surrounding them in the woods were super powerful, they wouldn't still be here under a bargain, working with so many other demons, and not killing the humans who'd released them from their containment circle.

They were still dangerous as all hell. Each one a potentially lethal threat. But...not the most powerful demons that could be summoned.

Still, there were a lot of them. Filling the woods with a red glow, the pervasive scent of sulfur competing with autumnal forest and the waxy scent of candles from the stone summoning circle.

A lot of demons for the humans to control.

Once a demon left a circle—breaking free or being set free, either counted—they lost a lot of power as well. Couldn't just walk into this realm without sacrificing power. At least not through a traditional summoning method. The more powerful the demon, the more power they sacrificed by cutting off the connection to their own realm.

They were still deadly. Even the least powerful of them. The average demon could rip through an average human in less than ten seconds without much effort. Still, leaving behind the tie to their own realm did cost them. The ones who wanted into this realm, for whatever reason, didn't actually care.

And the weaker the demon, the less power they sacrificed.

Was that why the men were calling less objectively powerful demons? Because they'd be sacrificing less power to come into this realm, where they would still be extremely dangerous?

Even if that was the reason, though, the question was still…why? Why do this at all? "Ruling" whatever that meant. But ruling what and whom and how?

And why?

Angie didn't understand the normal power grab motivations of a lot of humans. She didn't understand why people felt the need to have power over other people. The thought baffled her. But maybe that was because she had so much power, so much magical power to call on. She'd been trained to the "harm no other" principle as a guide for her life. She'd done harm of course—she ate food, including meat, she killed mosquitos and cockroaches, and sometimes things happened and you hurt someone on accident. The guide was impossible to follow perfectly. In fact, it was impossible to fully follow at all without dying of starvation because you refused to harm plants and animals.

But it was a helpful balance point in decision making. Especially for someone with Angie's level of power.

So she'd never understood the need to dominate and control others. But she recognized that she was a rare case. That others had this desire. The three dancing men likely did.

She just didn't get it.

"Rule who?" Angie asked the bat-winged demon, just to see if it would answer. Not that the answer had any real-world significance. Like Aidan implied, the whys mattered less than the getting-these-bastards-back-to-their-realms part did. But she wasn't sure the men who'd made all these demon-bargains would survive long enough to explain everything to her.

"Everyone," the demon hissed.

Well that didn't clarify anything at all.

"Careful talking to them," Sebastian said. "They'll twist your words into a bargain you didn't mean to make."

She scowled at the side of his face. She wanted to snap that she knew that. Except that she hadn't. *And whose fault was that, exactly, Angela.* The mental voice sounded entirely too much like her mother's.

"Okay," Aidan said, "here's what we're going to do." She finally looked away from the dancing men. "Angie, when I signal, drop the circle. I'll take the three men and the blue bastard about to be released. Sebastian, you handle the ones behind us. Angie, find a good tree while avoiding all contact with demons."

"Avoiding?" She glanced around. They were surrounded by demons. "I'm not sure that'll be possible."

"Sebastian and I will handle the demon fighting. You find a tree. Get ready. And…" Aidan met her gaze. "Brace. This won't be easy."

Angie nodded. She hadn't purposefully held open a portal into a demon realm before. Not on purpose. She'd only ever done it on accident. The on-purpose part seemed like a bad idea.

But it was why she was here. And with all these demons on the loose, it *was* the easiest way to get them back into a demon realm.

It did occur to her to wonder how the hunters would have handled all these escaped demons at once without her here to open a breech between the realms. But she decided not to ask while they had a demon audience.

She glanced at the bat-winged demons again. The middle one was still doing that thing with its face that might have been a smile but also might have just been it baring its teeth at her. Ugh. So many teeth.

How the hell was she going to avoid demons to search for the right tree?

She kept the trigger word for her second spell at the front of her mind, and waited for Aidan's signal to cut the circle.

Moments ticked by, making Angie's palms sweat, her heartbeat already hammered, slamming against her ribcage, but now she felt the anxiety and anticipation in her throat, in her gut. Clawing at her to get out on a scream.

"Now!"

Angie cut the circle.

Aidan raced to the circle and the chanting humans. Sebastian dove toward the bat-winged trio. And Angie…

For a heartbeat, she froze. Surrounded by demons, no idea how they'd get out of this, and aware that she wasn't doing her part.

She watched Sebastian drop and rolling into the middle of the demons, coming up on his feet in their midst. The move had all three turning rapidly to face him, moving with more coordinated grace than she'd expected. They swarmed toward him, but he tossed one into another and ducked under the third as if they were dolls and he was playing a game.

The ease with which he handled the bat-winged demons snapped Angie from her frozen panic. She ducked a little—she had no idea why—and moved around the edge of the clearing, just a few yards, looking for the tree, the one with the natural V formed by its trunk, the tree she could use.

To tear a breach into the demon world.

CHAPTER FOUR

*A*ngie bumped off a solid pine trunk as she made her way around the inside of the treeline, the spindly offshoot branches scrapping against her jacket. The scent of pine resin was strong in this section of the woods, but she'd spotted a couple of gambel oak trees that just might work. Careful not to look at the naturally formed Vs, at least not into them, she still had to find one that would work for the sheer number of demons running around the clearing. Something big enough for all these bastards to fit through.

The surroundings were filled with the screeching screaming hiss of demons. She didn't dare look at the hunters and their fights for too long and get distracted. But from the corner of her eye, she was aware of Aidan physically fighting with the three men while simultaneously preventing the blue demon from escaping—it wasn't out of the circle so Angie assumed Aidan was doing that—and ducking away from the other demons attacking her while she tried to deal with the men who'd summoned them.

Sebastian was still tossing the bat-winged demons around, but they'd been joined by two other demons which set the odds against him.

Angie was so tempted to trigger her spell, but feared distracting the hunters. They had their knowledge and their wills to fight demons. Distracting someone using their will the way a hunter did was dangerous…to the hunter.

Then Sebastian pulled a sword from somewhere. One moment he was physically fighting demons. The next he held a long sword in two hands, the blade thick and covered in red-hot flames.

What the…?

Demon hunters used swords? That was something Aidan hadn't mentioned.

She looked to Aidan, but she wasn't using any weapons. Just herself. She was chanting now, something that must have upset the humans because they dove at her. Between one moment and the next, Aidan seemed to disappear. And then she was there again. A few feet away, chanting once more. As the humans looked around in confusion.

Angie shook off her own distraction and returned to the tree hunt. The longer she watched them fight, the longer they'd have to fight.

The perfect tree rose up from the surrounding woods suddenly, almost as if it had materialized there just where she needed it. That flight of fancy had her shaking her head. Silly witch. But the size of the Rocky Mountain maple trunk and the V-shape formed when the trunk split and grew in two different directions was perfect.

Almost in the same instant she found the tree, though, a bat-winged demon dove from above, aiming at her head. She ducked instinctively. Spun to face it as it swooped between the trees, screeched, and dove at her again. She murmured a few words and cut her fingers in a sharp gesture, then flung her hands up in front of her.

A strong wind blew the bat-winged demon up into the tree branches, sending a shower of pine needles to the ground. The trees captured and tangled the demon up, long enough for Angie to breathe.

Barely.

Then another demon, this one of the larger ones with molten lava skin, stepped in front of her.

Damn it, she wasn't supposed to be facing demons. Aidan had said to avoid them. Spells and her kind of magic took time. And she had no hand-to-hand training. She could throw a punch because she'd grown up with brothers and their mother had made them all learn how to throw a proper punch without breaking their thumbs. But she didn't want to get close enough to the lava demon to touch its skin—skin that would melt her fragile human body—nonetheless punch the bastard.

She was about to trigger her last stored spell, the failsafe still waiting for her to call it. Then Sebastian was between her and the lava demon. One moment he hadn't been there. The next he was.

Blinking in shock, she did another unfortunate freeze,

unable to process the reality of him being there for a full forty seconds. Which didn't sound like long, but in a fight with a demon was an eternity.

He swung that giant flame encased sword at the lava demon. It went through the beast like butter, opening the center of the demon up so that the lava dripped down its front like blood.

The demon roared and threw itself backward. More lava dripped to the ground, catching some of the dry needles and grass on fire. Angie cursed quietly before murmuring another spell.

Aloud, she said, "Sorry about this." Then triggered the spell. Rain dumped out of the sky.

There had only been a few clouds close enough and not nearly enough moisture in the air for her rain spell to create much of a shower, but it was enough to put out the small fires created by the demon's wound.

"Good option," Sebastian said, grinning at her over his shoulder.

She blinked a few times. For a split second, she was tempted to smile back.

Then the men who'd summoned the demons started cursing loudly and Angie shook herself back to the situation.

Dangerous. Losing track of her surroundings because of a stunning smile in a too-handsome face.

The lava demon lunged at them again. Before Angie could shout a warning, Sebastian had his sword up.

He forced the demon away from her, shouting, "Get ready. It's almost time."

She couldn't tell if his sword or his will did most of the work driving the demon back, but she'd guess both.

She spun toward the tree she knew would work, keeping her gaze lowered enough not to accidentally look into the V too soon. She'd get caught and be helpless once she did, especially if she wanted to hold the damned breach open. She couldn't afford to have that happen before she was ready.

Not that she was ever ready. She hated all of this. A lot.

She glanced back at Sebastian. Maybe not all of it.

Hunting for Aidan, she saw her standing between the three men and a row of demons—three of the bat-winged creatures and the one gray and tentacled beast. The gray was in the center and a little forward, the leader, and it was smiling at Aidan with rows and rows of sharp sharp teeth. That one had a more human adjacent face, so the expressions were easier to read. Not pleasant. But easier.

"You can't banish us all, hunter," the gray said. "We will have this world."

Aidan shrugged, as if this wasn't a horrifyingly terrible situation. And when the gray lurched at her, she didn't even flinch. She stood her ground and stared at it, and when it tried to reach for her, its tentacles hit an invisible wall. The demon hissed and drew its tentacles closer around its body.

Aidan chuckled. Actually chuckled!

"My will is stronger than yours," she said.

"No mere human's will is stronger than mine," the gray hissed.

"You'd be wrong there. And it's time to go back. You're not welcome here."

One of the bat-winged creatures screeched so loudly Angie covered her ears. Ouch. The sound was high and piercing and cut right through her despite her hands. And wow, why was that making the stench of sulfur stronger?

She looked around. Sebastian held off three demons—the lava, a bat-winged beast, and another tentacled creature that was a different species to the gray. Angie wanted to help him, but didn't know what to do that wouldn't distract him.

All of it came down to will—according to Aidan. And she'd just watched Aidan deflect a demon attack without moving, without magic. With only her will. Will, the way demon hunters used it, sort of looked like magic, though. From the outside. If they survived this, Angie was going to ask more about that.

The gray laughed at Aidan and lunged at her again. It smashed up against her will, will she was using to create a shield of some kind—at least that's what it looked like to Angie's magic trained gaze—and the creature screeched in frustrated response.

One of the men at Aidan's back raised a knife. Angie opened her mouth to call a warning, but Aidan raised a hand in her direction, almost as if she'd known what Angie was about to do and was quieting her. Then the human drew the knife down across his own arm, releasing a line of blood.

Angie had cut herself only once for a spell. It hurt like a bitch. She hated blood magic so avoided it. That sort of spellcraft wasn't her specialty anyway.

The blood distracted the demons. All the demons in the woods. Including the bat-winged beast who was swooping overhead and heading toward Angie. She ducked as it changed directions, but it hadn't actually gotten close enough to grab at her. Thankfully, since she hadn't seen it coming.

Fuck, she was out of her depth here.

Another rain spell would be nice, at least provide them some cover. But there wasn't enough moisture in the surroundings, and if she pulled out too much, she'd dry the trees and maybe even start a forest fire. They didn't need that. Wind worked against the winged beasts, but she was pretty sure it would have no effect on the other demons.

She had a shield spell that might help, but she was still perfecting it and was afraid she'd screw it up if she tried it under these circumstances. She had a confusion spell, a spark spell—which required her to get too close to the demons for her comfort—and a few others that were not suited to combat.

Especially with immortal beings they couldn't kill.

One of the few things she did know about demons was that humans couldn't kill them. Not even a demon hunter. The hunters sent them back to their realms. They cut them off from this realm. But they couldn't kill them.

She had a moment to wonder about Sebastian's sword. Could it kill a demon? That seemed unlikely. If there was a weapon humans could use to kill them, there'd be more of those weapons about. Every hunter would want one.

Then the man who'd released some of his own blood started to chant again. A spell this time. Like a witch's spell.

One Angie recognized.

Oh. This was not good.

CHAPTER FIVE

anic clenched Angie's throat. The bastard who'd cut his arm and was now chanting was working a witch's binding spell. A *binding* spell.

There were two kinds of binding spells. One, the kind that bound up another magic practitioner's magic. Kept that magic caged, shackled, so that they couldn't use it. Those spells were hard to pull off if the witch or wizard was strong enough. It took a lot of resources and time and patience and skill to bind another practitioner's magic. The bound magic wielder could, with enough skill, eventually break most binding spells. And there were consequences to the caster. There had to be a serious reason to do that kind of binding, because doing so also bound up the caster's magic. It meant the person casting the spell could no longer use their own magic either.

The chanting man was not attempting that.

The other kind of binding spell involved tying oneself to another person. At least in humans. Binding a human to another human meant they were so tightly linked that when one was hurt, the other felt it, and when one had power, the other could use it. They could see through each other's eyes, they could hear through each other's ears, they could speak through each other's voices.

Sometimes the binding spells were temporary, a way for two close people to stay…entangled while separated or while working a particular kind of magic together. Very very few were permanent because, really, who would want to be permanently entangled with someone else so that you felt their pain and suffering and, maybe worse, they felt yours.

But those types of spells existed and were occasionally used. The spell the chanting man was invoking with his blood was that second kind of spell.

He wasn't attempting to bind himself to another human, though.

He was binding himself to one of the demons.

A spell that would tie him to one of the demons? That sort of thing seemed… Stupid was maybe too kind a word. Suicidal more like.

She had no idea what binding himself to a demon would actually do. The very idea of something like that had never crossed her mind. What would happen to him if he was still bound to the demon once it was back in its own realm? Could he even accomplish this?

Fuck, she had no clue.

She could disrupt his spell, try to prevent him from casting. But doing so would have consequences she couldn't predict. Magic was a bitch that way. Calling it took a lot of control and messing up in mid-casting had a lot of potential for disasters.

"Aidan," she called, because she needed to warn the hunter. "He's trying to bind himself to a demon."

Maybe Aidan would know how to stop him.

Angie's last spell, the one still hovering in her mind, ready to trigger, could make thing worse here. It was an illusion spell. A distraction spell. She'd designed it to keep the demons confused so the hunters could send them back to the demon realm easier. But confused demons chasing hallucinations while bound to a human… Seemed potentially disastrous.

Aidan didn't curse out loud, but her mouth turned down in a frown Angie recognized. An irritated and frustrated expression rare for the hunter.

Sebastian startled a yelp out of Angie by appearing next to her suddenly. "Don't do that!" Angie snarled at him.

"Sorry. The binding spell? What demon is he attempting to bind to?"

"Got me. I don't know the names of all these demons, so I can't tell which one he's invoking. He's calling it a…"

She listened a moment longer. The chant was a mix of Latin and English, and it was hard to distinguish the demon's identity among the Latin. She knew the spell, what type and flavor it was, but not well enough she could have invoked it herself. Which meant she didn't have all the words memorized, and that complicated parsing out the demon's species.

"…a Bakka demon. I think. That's not Latin or English, the languages he's using in the spell. It's the only word I don't recognize."

"Old English word for bat."

"He's binding himself to one of the bat-winged bastards? Why?" And which one? There were easily a dozen of them.

"Good question. No answers."

"Helpful." She sucked in a breath. "If I open the portal now, can you and Aidan drive the demons through before he's finished."

"Portal?"

"No time to explain."

Sebastian looked like he wanted to ask more but knew she was right about the time. "How close is he to being finished?"

"Too close. Another few minutes." The good and bad thing about a witch's spellcasting was that it took time. Not instantaneous magic. No wizard bolts and energy bolts to call quickly and use as weapons. But witch magic, once cast, could pack a serious punch.

In this instant, if the man finished, that would be bad.

"Right." Sebastian almost absently sliced his sword to one side, knocking an incoming bat-winged demon up and back, sending it screeching into the trees. One of the lava-skinned creatures was heading toward Aidan. And the other two men responsible for this mess had worked around to the other side of the still-bound blue blob demon, which meant they were attempting to free it again.

Bad enough they had all these different demons to worry about, but the three humans working against them just made everything worse.

The gray tentacled demon managed to slither up behind Aidan, though when it lurched at her, it came up hard against her will and froze in place.

If Angie had a shield that worked that good against demons, she'd have it cast all the time. But Angie didn't have the will of a demon hunter. Her will was strong, or she couldn't control her own magic, but different to the will of a hunter, different to the will Aidan was exerting to hold off the demons converging on her.

"We have to help her," Angie said. "We have to do something."

The second sentence wasn't even out of her mouth before Sebastian was off. But he didn't head toward Aidan. He ran, sword at his side, toward the men at the back of the stone circle. And the three bat-winged demons coming up behind them.

Too many demons. Three humans working to free more. Only two hunters. And her.

And she was in over her head.

She watched in horror as the freed demons in the clearing all converged on the stone circle, on the three humans and two hunters. None of them were coming for her anymore. That gave her breathing space, but also too much room to panic as she watched things unfold and didn't know how to help.

Distraction. That would have to do. The demons needed to be distracted from the hunters.

"I'm triggering the second spell," she shouted at Aidan in warning.

The hunter's only response was a slight lift of her hand, but she hadn't taken her gaze off the man who'd cut himself and was attempting a binding with a demon.

Angie, let out a long breath, murmured the last word of her spell and made the last hand gesture to release it.

For a long moment, nothing happened. Angie watched as Sebastian engaged the gray tentacled demon with his sword. As Aidan raised a hand to hold back the bat-winged being that dropped toward her. As the man who was invoking the binding spell looked up and smiled.

And then…

Fireworks.

Well, some fireworks. And sparkles. And a myriad of running rainbows. And butterflies that glowed in the dark.

All dancing around the clearing.

The moment's pause. The looks of confusion from the human men. The way the demons turned to swat at the dancing, shimmering lights.

Angie might have laughed if there hadn't been so many demons still free and wandering around.

The man who'd been about to set his binding spell fell silent as he spun in a tight circle, taking in the flashes of light and noise. The fireworks sounded like fireworks, high pitched whistles followed by pops and crackles and sizzles and occasional booms. The sparkles came with a little whizzing sizzle of their own. The running rainbows sang a song every time they jumped past.

The only silent things were the illuminated butterflies which flittered suddenly around in front of everyone, seeming to come out of nowhere and ignoring all efforts to brush them away.

"Now," Aidan called.

Angie didn't hesitate. She probably should have. She hadn't really braced for this. But they only had this narrow window.

She faced the tree with the natural V in its trunk and looked through that V…

Into a demon realm.

CHAPTER SIX

The realm beyond the V in the tree trunk was a fire and brimstone kind of place. Volcanic activity far off in the distance. The sound of black ground tinkling like glass as it cooled over rivers of rolling, red hot lava. Heat pulsed in the air, shimmering eddies distorting the views beyond. The stench of sulfur reached her, faint at first, then almost overwhelming as the rotten egg flavor coated her tongue.

Angie swallowed her revulsion and kept her gaze on the realm breach she'd opened.

As long as she stared, the portal stayed open. As long as she kept her gaze on the space between the V, things could move between the realms. Even without looking at it, she was always aware of these holes, these thin places, where the barriers between realms were little more than tissue paper.

But until she looked directly, until she poked a hole in the tissue paper with her gaze, the barrier held. Nothing got through.

No one even noticed the thinness was there.

Her gaze highlighted it, broke it open. And let the demons on the other side *see* her. See the opening. She wasn't sure why her gaze opened a portal into demon realms. She didn't care much about the whys. She cared about controlling the ability—curse?—and *not* opening these breaches. Ever.

Except now, when the hunters, when Aidan had called on her for help, she couldn't refuse. And she couldn't help in any better way than this.

But the hunters had to drive the demons through. She couldn't do both.

The breach caught her, the compulsion or spell or whatever it was kept her staring at the opening, unable to look away. She didn't dare look away yet, but instinct made her want to. She wanted to tear her gaze from that stinking, red, hot realm so badly she shook. Fisting her hands, she held her ground even as the first bat-winged beast flew past her with an ear-piercing screech.

It crashed through the tree, sucked back into the demon realm with a gross slurping noise that made her want to gag. Why did the process have to sound so disgusting?

Another creature, this one of the lava-skinned monsters, suddenly filled the V between the tree trunk. It scrambled at the air in front of it, but the realm beyond still sucked it through, retaking it. Like to like.

They would try to escape again, through the hole Angie

held open. Even as another bat-winged creature flew into the breach, the first was attempting to fly out again. They could see the opening, they could return, but Angie couldn't take her gaze off the breach to close it and lock them out yet. Not until the rest had been driven through.

She wanted to look away and see what Aidan and Sebastian were doing. She heard some shouts. Heard Sebastian yell something. Another bat-winged beast raced past in her peripheral vision, spinning at the last minute as it attempted to avoid the gateway back to its realm.

It might have been able to avoid getting sucked through if tentacles from beyond the breach hadn't shot out just then to grab the bat-winged demon. The demon shrieked and struggled. The tentacles pulled and jerked the demon back into the hellscape.

The gray beast reappeared inside the V. It smiled, with all its rows of sharp sharp teeth, its momentum from flinging the bat-winged creature behind it carrying it half out of the portal again. Only for it to be hit in the face by the second lava demon slamming into it. That carried both demons back through.

Angie let out a breath.

More demons went through. She lost count, her focus on holding the portal. How many more? How many were left? Had the blue blob demon been released? Had the witch binding himself to one of the demons finished his spell or abandoned it? Were Sebastian and Aidan all right?

Questions she couldn't answer. She wanted to close the portal and lock in the beasts that kept trying to get back out.

But Aidan hadn't shouted the signal. Even without that, Angie was aware there were still demons behind her, screeching their protests.

She was so focused on her part, on keeping the portal open, ensuring the other demons could be tossed through, the sudden appearance of Sebastian at her side startled a yelp out of her. She'd be embarrassed about that later.

He swung his sword up and over her head and another bat-winged beast went through the gap in the tree, crashing into the demons already there as they attempted to climb out again.

Angie let out another little sound, but she wasn't sure what the sound meant. Combination of startled and grateful for Sebastian's help and worried about what had almost just happened, what would have happened if he hadn't been there.

"How are you doing this?" he murmured. "What are you doing?"

"Get the rest through," she managed between clenched teeth.

She couldn't explain now. It took all she had to keep the gateway open while not losing herself. She had to hold onto herself so she could close the breach. To be able to pull back from the compulsion to stare and hold it open.

She fingered the pentagram hanging from her bracelet, letting the cold metal pattern ground her, keep her inside herself. A little shiver of its protective magic vibrated through her fingers. She pressed the charm tighter.

Sebastian stared at the side of her face a moment longer, glanced back at the tree just as the green-scaled demon tried to crawl back into this realm. Sebastian swiped the reaching tentacles and the demon screamed in protest as one of its limbs landed in a steaming heap on the forest floor.

The green disappeared back inside the hellscape, and Sebastian left his spot by her side.

Another bat-winged beast flew past her head. How many left now? She hadn't seen a blue blob demon in her peripheral vision had she? Was the one in the circle still contained?

More shouting from behind her. A human scream that didn't bode well. She wanted to look. She wanted to help.

She couldn't turn her back on the gateway she'd opened.

A moment of noise, shouting, another human scream, and then to her surprise, a blue blob demon went barreling past her, as if of its own according, running toward the breach between realms the way demons from the other side kept trying to charge into this one. The blue demon roared, a sound like a cross between a lion and an elephant, but deeper and with a hiss at the end. No sound an animal in this realm could make.

In its hurry to go through the open gateway, it knocked her sideways. Angie stumbled and nearly looked away from the tree too soon, before the demon got through. Strong hands caught her shoulders, holding her in place, keeping her upright until she could find her own footing.

"How many are left?" she breathed.

"That was the last," Sebastian said near her ear.

"Close it," Aidan called. "Now."

Angie pressed her lips together, tightened her hold on the

pentagram. The pervasive stench of sulfur coated her throat. She focused on the coolness at her back, at the warm hands gripping her shoulders, the much more pleasant scent of Sebastian. She leaned into him, and with an effort that wrenched, dropped her gaze.

The sounds of protests and screeches from the demon realm echoed in her mind.

CHAPTER SEVEN

Keeping her gaze down, Angie turned away from the maple tree with its convenient V-shaped trunk. The movement brought her face to face with Sebastian. They locked gazes, and for a long moment she felt as compelled to hold his gaze as she'd felt staring into the other realm.

She didn't dare reach up and touch him. She felt too raw and was afraid she'd accidentally read something from him. Which would feel like an invasion of privacy in that moment. Bad enough he was touching her, but she was better at controlling that kind of contact, preventing an unintentional reading.

Despite knowing she shouldn't touch him, though, she very much wanted to reach up and cup his cheek. The impulse left her a little breathless.

"Are you willing to explain?" he asked quietly, a mere murmur. "What you did? What happened there?"

"Aidan didn't tell you?"

He shook his head.

"I'll explain. But not here." He was a hunter and there was no point in not telling him. Aidan would when he asked anyway, she was sure.

She was a little surprised Aidan hadn't already told him, though. Explained why she'd bring a witch on a hunt. Angie would ask Aidan about that.

But not here.

She finally dragged her gaze away from Sebastian. The wrench less painful than pulling away from a demon realm, but strangely just as disorienting. She was still acutely aware of his hands on her shoulders as she hunted the clearing for Aidan and the other humans.

One of the men, the one who'd been invoking the binding spell, was flat out on the ground, his hands against his head, panting and shaking and muttering something under his breath. The other two men were on the ground next to him. One had a hand over his arm, and a little blood leaked through his fingers. The other had his head between his hands. He almost looked asleep.

For the first time, Angie really looked at the men, taking in their appearances. Each seemed a lot younger now than she'd thought at first. Close to her age, early twenties, maybe younger even. The witch who'd conjured the binding spell didn't look old enough to have the control for such a spell. From the looks of him now, he probably hadn't.

"The binding spell?" Sebastian asked.

"I'm not sure what it's doing to him," she said, "but he finished it. So he's linked to…one of the demons."

"Still?"

"Still. And the demon he's bound to is in a demon realm now."

The man screamed then, a piercing noise that made Angie wince.

"That seems like a bad sort of binding," Sebastian said.

"Yup."

She headed toward the witch, ignoring her twinge of regret at the loss of contact with Sebastian. She wasn't sure she could help. She hadn't ever learned how to break a binding spell a witch had invoked on themselves. But despite the idiot's efforts to unleash demons on this realm—and she would love an explanation for that stupidity—she didn't want to leave him as he was. The binding would likely kill him, but probably drive him insane before that.

Aidan stepped from the shadows at the edge of the trees and fell into step next to Angie. "Woods are clear," she said. "You okay?"

"Been better," Angie admitted. "I haven't done that in years."

"You did good."

Angie snorted. Good? Well, the demons had gone through and were still on the other side without a whole host of them running loose in this realm, so she supposed that was good.

They all stopped to stare down at the demon-bound witch. His eyes were wide open, the pupils shrunk to a pinpoint leaving almost all dark brown iris and lots of white. His white skin was so pale he looked nearly translucent in the dim light from the candles still remarkably flickering around the stone circle. Sweat beaded his forehead and upper lip.

He screamed suddenly, sharply. The sound made everyone but the hunters jump.

"Help him," one of the men on the ground demanded.

Aidan raised a brow at him. He was another white man, his hair a pale enough brown to be almost blond, his features sharp and angular. He was the one with the slice on his arm that he mostly ignored.

"He did this to himself," Aidan said. "And I'm not a witch."

Angie sighed. She was. But she didn't know how to help him.

"This is your fault," the man with the cut hissed. "Do something."

"You're not helping your case, mate," Sebastian said quietly, a rumble of anger in his response that wasn't in Aidan's.

"You cut him?" Angie asked.

"I did," Sebastian said with no evident regret.

"You want something to stop the bleeding?" she asked the man just to see how he'd respond.

"Fuck you."

Okay. So not worried about the fact that he could bleed out.

During all this, the second conscious man kept his head in his hands, never once looking up. Angie could barely tell what he looked like except that he had shaggy brown hair and his hands were pale and trembling.

Aidan leaned close to her and murmured, "Anything you can do?" She nodded down at the man who'd bound himself to a demon. "He's an idiot, but…"

Yeah, Angie got it. Even an idiot probably didn't deserve what was happening in that man's head at the moment. He screamed again, raw and loud, and while she didn't jump this time, she did flinch.

"Not sure there's anything I can do." That wouldn't kill him anyway. But she didn't say that out loud. She could brute force break his spell, maybe. But the consequences to his mind weren't likely to be good. And her attempt to break a spell by brute force might not even work. She was a strong magic wielder, but still needed a lot of training. She wasn't sure she trusted her skills with this unknown.

"Could you try?" Aidan said. "Leaving him like this…" She gestured just as he screamed again. "He won't survive much longer."

"Stupid to have done the spell in the first place," Angie muttered. She leaned over the man, keeping a little distance because he was thrashing around now, arms and legs flailing, his eyes rolled back into his head so only the whites showed.

This was not good. She hovered her hands over him, but the twisting magics of his spell were…fuzzy and unclear that way. She had to touch him.

She did not want to touch him.

"I have to touch him," she murmured out loud to make herself do it.

She was a little surprised when Sebastian stepped up behind her. "I'm here to pull you away if you need me to," he murmured. So quietly she wasn't sure even Aidan would have heard him.

She nodded a little to show she'd heard. Then gently set her hands on the thrashing man's chest. She didn't open her psychic skills fully. There was a lot she just didn't want to know about this guy. But she opened a tiny bit. Enough to feel the magic in the spell and tease it out. There had to be a way to do this without using her psychic abilities, but she didn't know that way. Something she'd need to learn. This would do for now.

Even that little crack in her psychic senses was enough to confirm she didn't want to read more. Some people's minds and lives were just too… They were the stuff of nightmares, and she had enough of those all her own.

The spell did come clearer, though. She'd heard a lot of it as he was invoking it, so reversing it might be possible. She followed the currents of power, the way the lines of the spell made a pattern in her mind's eye. The knotted loops of blue wrapped around the man, lines of that blue running toward the tree where she'd formed the portal to the hellscape. But more of those lines reaching out and around him. In all different directions. Down into the ground, away from the tree, toward the sky. All around, like he was surrounded by spikes of magical light linking him to everything.

She was pretty sure that wasn't what he'd intended with the spell.

She nudged one of the many lines where it connected to

the knot that, in her otherworldy vision, occupied most of the center of him. He screamed. Okay. Not good. She tried another line, giving it a very gentle tug at the place where it met the knot of his spell. He thrashed harder and let out a scream so loud she winced.

"Stop it! You're killing him," the wounded man said.

"You told her to do this," Aidan pointed out reasonably. "Now you tell her to stop. She might not be able to help him at all, which means he'll die. And it'll be his own doing."

Aidan's calm, reasonable assessment left Angie feeling a little better, and she wasn't sure why. Maybe Aidan was willing her some calm. That would be nice. She needed more calm. Because every time the man screamed, it set her nerves jumping and her heart racing. Without some measure of calm, she wasn't going to be able to help him, even a little bit. And yet her attempts to help him were shattering her nerves.

Another wave of...something washed through her and calmed her nerves further, let her center a little better. Huh. Didn't feel like magic. Might almost feel like her own inner strength serving up a little calming wash of hormones. But this didn't feel like her. This felt like it came from outside her.

She nudged yet another line in the knot. This time the man didn't scream. His body bowed up and his muscles tightened. But he didn't scream in agony. That had to count as progress. She mentally took hold of that line of magic and tugged. The man panted, clenched his jaw. That was obviously pain, but still no screaming. Good. She tugged again.

Under her breath, she began a spell designed to reverse bad magic. She wasn't sure if this was the right spell in this case. There was probably an unbinding spell somewhere. She'd just never studied it. But since this was definitely a bad use of magic, she hoped the reverse of bad magic would do something for her. Bonus, the spell didn't require hand gestures until the very end, which meant she could keep the physical contact with the man. Helpful as she continued to study the knot of threads binding him to the demon.

The one that she could tug without making him scream led to the very heart of the knot. She tugged gently again as she came close to the end of her spell. The man's muscles all tightened and his teeth clacked together as he clenched his jaw. She should probably stop now, but she continued to tug at the thread as she finished her chant, taking her hands from the man's chest only long enough to form the final gestures. Then she sent the spell into the knot.

She watched the pattern of blue thread loosen. Not unravel, but loosen. Loosen enough for her to following the thread she held into the center of the knot. Good. That was something.

At the center was a little glowing ball of red. That would be the demon link. She didn't want to touch that. Not even a little. Opening a portal for the first time in years was bad enough. Close enough contact with the demon realms. She'd have to unravel the knot fully without touching that red orb.

Easier said than done. She kept her eyes closed as she

worked, trusting Aidan—and strangely Sebastian—to have her back. In fact, having Sebastian literally at her back, guarding her and ready to pull her out of this if things went sideways was…maybe a little too reassuring. A little too much like relief. And also, for reasons she didn't dare look at too closely, made her feel a little fizz of happiness in her gut.

That was absolutely something she didn't have time to deal with right now. The strange giddy dance in her tummy just thinking about Sebastian would be better faced later.

She unraveled a few of the threads, pulling them completely free of the knot. The minute they were released, they dissolved, the magic spilling away into the ground beneath the man. She let it go. He was in no shape to reintegrate the used magic back into himself anyway. Plus, she was sure there was demon taint on that magic. The man was better off without it.

She wasn't entirely sure why she cared. He'd summoned a fuck load of demons and had then gone and bound himself to one. Not only was this his own fault, he'd been engaged in an evil act. She didn't really care about him on an emotional level that she could explain. She just wanted to break his spell and free him from the torture.

He screamed again, but she was so deep into the magic at that point, she barely heard him. And his thrashing was weaker now, so she wasn't in danger of losing physical contact with him. Although she might be in danger of losing him period. Part of her still wondered why the hell he'd done all this. Part of her didn't really care.

She worked through another, trickier thread in the knot,

and with a mentally audible pop, something gave. The entire knot unraveled in front of her mind's eye. The red, pulsing orb at the center of the knot flared brightly and a rush of heat washed over her, like stepping out into the summer desert heat from an overly airconditioned store. Dry and breath-stealing and surprisingly, weirdly pleasant.

That last made her wince. Nothing to do with demons should be pleasant. Especially not their heat. The fact that it was, that she'd liked that wash of heat, was worrisome.

She waited until the pulsing red dot shrunk and vanished before she finally opened her eyes and reoriented to the real world. The man under her hands was still now, his eyes closed. But he was breathing, so she hadn't accidentally killed him unraveling his spell. That was something, she supposed.

"I should be studying for my midterms," she murmured, mostly to herself.

Sebastian stepped closer, and she felt his hand hovering over her shoulder. But he didn't touch her. And a moment later, he stepped away again.

"He's separated from the demon now?" Aidan asked.

"Mostly. Not clear what kind of damage was ultimately caused. But the bond is broken."

"Thank you," the injured man said, his voice gruff.

She glared at him. "Why the fuck did you summon so damned many demons? What the fuck did that get you?" Her anger rose as she asked, even though she wasn't expecting an answer.

She wasn't disappointed. The man glared back at her and

kept his mouth shut. The second man didn't even glance up, hadn't glanced up throughout all the screaming and yelling. Angie was starting to wonder if he was even conscious.

"They're part of a…cult would be the best word," Aidan said.

Surprising Angie and the man both because the man turned his glare on Aidan.

"End of the world cult," Aidan said. "Summon lots of demons. Release them on the world. Ensure you're bound to a demon so you have power over the remaining humans. Apocalyptic fantasy world for them to play in."

Angie cursed again. "Well that's a fucking shit idea."

Sebastian huffed a sound like a laugh but not quite.

"These three came the closest to unleashing more demons than they could handle," Aidan said. "The others have been…stopped earlier than this."

"Why were they allowed to get this far?" Angie demanded.

"Not allowed. Got to this point before we could get here." Aidan shrugged. "We can't all teleport."

The phrasing brought Angie blinking up short. Wait. Some of the hunters could teleport?

Aidan grinned.

Angie couldn't tell if she was joking or not with that grin. She decided to believe it was a joke because Aidan had a very weird sense of humor.

"How do you know this?" the injured man growled.

"It's my job," Aidan said. "Sorry we dragged you into it, though," she said to Angie, mostly ignoring the injured man.

"But I am glad you were here." She gestured to the now unconscious man. "Neither of us could have done anything to help him with a magic spell."

Demon hunters didn't wield magic. Even if the way they could use their will did sometimes look like magic. She wondered if Aidan was being honest, though. She didn't know enough about exactly what the hunters could do with their will to say for sure that they couldn't use it to break a magical spell. In fact, she suspected they'd have to be able to use it against magic because demons possessed a kind of magic. Their power manifested as "magic" in this realm anyway. Fighting demon magic meant the hunters *could* fight magic. But maybe they couldn't break anything that wasn't demonic? Maybe witch magic was beyond their will?

And did Angie really want to know the answers to those questions? She was curious enough to say yes, but had enough self-preservation instincts to know that if she got those answers, it might drag her in too deep into the hunters' world for her own good. Probably better to remain on the outside, and let them keep their secrets.

She glanced back at Sebastian and something like regret moved through her. She ignored it.

"Now what?" she asked Aidan.

"We go."

"What about them?" Angie nodded to the cult members who'd just nearly brought about a mini-apocalypse.

"They have some recovering to do." Aidan got into the face of the injured man, so suddenly he leaned backward and blinked hard. Aidan smiled at him. "I wouldn't recommend continuing to summon demons, though. We'll be here next time. And the time after that. And we'll keep stopping you from unleashing them on the world. It's what we do. But… Who knows if next time we can stop them from claiming you. We won't always have someone with us who can break a binding spell. Ask him when he comes to what it was like. Then rethink your life. And maybe, maybe…get a new set of friends. Up to you of course."

She straightened away from the man, who was trying to glare at her, but his gaze kept darting to his unconscious associate.

The third man finally glanced up from under the scruff of his hair, giving Angie a narrow view of dark eyes with heavy purple circles underneath.

"And if that's not warning enough," Aidan continued to the injured man, "I do believe there are some people in law enforcement that have a great deal of interest in what your friends have been doing. More than you might realize. They will have some questions for you. If you don't stop heading down this road."

Angie stood away from the unconscious man, watching the injured one working through everything Aidan was telling him. His expression was still mulishly stubborn. Maybe he'd take the advice. Maybe he wouldn't.

But either way, it was no longer her problem. The hunters could deal with these idiots.

As they turned to leave though, Angie did say, "Definitely ask him what that bond with a demon was like. What it did to him." She sighed. "If he wakes up, he's going to need a hospital or a healer. I'm not a healer, so I couldn't fix the…damage."

This got the injured man blinking. He scurried closer to his associate on the ground, pressing a hand to his chest.

Angie followed Aidan, Sebastian at her back, as they left the three men to clean up their mess. If they could.

CHAPTER EIGHT

The diner was quiet this time of night, only a few scattered people sitting at booths at the opposite side of the open dining room and one person sitting at the counter. There weren't any people at the free-standing tables in the middle of the room, which gave them even more space and privacy.

Angie worked her way through her burger and fries, feeling like she hadn't eaten in a month. After working all that magic to unravel the binding spell right after opening a demon realm portal took its toll on her strength. And now that she no longer had the stink of sulfur in her nose, her hunger overwhelmed her. She drank three refilled sodas and had nearly finished her meal before anyone spoke.

Sebastian sat across the table from her, Aidan next to him. He'd ordered a burger and fries too, and was mostly done eating when Angie finally pushed her plate away. Aidan had finished her bowl of spaghetti and side of fries a few minutes before Angie and was nursing a Coke.

"Spaghetti at a diner?" Angie asked.

Aidan shrugged. "This place makes a good red sauce."

Angie let out a half-hearted chuckle.

"Thanks for helping tonight," Aidan said.

"You're welcome."

"Do you want to explain?" Aidan nodded to Sebastian. "Or I can later."

Angie glanced around the diner. No one was close enough to overhear if they spoke quietly. But even if someone was close enough, she was pretty sure Aidan could just will them not to hear.

"Not a lot to explain," she said to Sebastian, who was staring at her. For a beat, she forgot she was supposed to be talking, getting lost in that stare, those lovely dark eyes, with just a faint hint of red in the depths. She blinked and shook her head. "I can open portals to demon realms, realm breaches if you will. All I need is a tree trunk that forms a natural V. Doesn't happen with just branches. Needs to be the actual trunk of the tree. Has to have grown that way, to form the V-shape naturally."

"How? Magic? A spell?"

"No. At least nothing active like that. It's magic, I guess. But not anything I control. I just have to…look through the tree, and I can see into a demon realm. And my looking thins the barrier between that realm and this one."

"Thins it?"

"Enough the demons can see the opening. Enough to let things out," she said quietly.

"But also enough to force things back," Aidan added.

Angie shrugged, but she didn't look away from Sebastian.

"I didn't see anything," Sebastian said. "But the demons that went through disappeared."

"Unless they get out into this realm, no one sees what I see. Not through the tree, anyway. You'd see the demons after they broke through the breach I opened. I'm the only one who has the..." She was about to say, with heavy sarcasm, the "pleasure" of seeing into the realms. But she pulled back on her ire. Sebastian didn't deserve her sarcasm right now. None of this was his fault.

Not anyone's fault really. It was a curse-gift she had and had to deal with. Life wasn't fair. But that didn't mean she had to like it.

She finished her sentence with, "I'm the only one who sees into the realm."

"When did you first discover you could do that?" He kept his voice quiet and low, the English accent a calming rumble.

"Five. Church parking lot." She finally looked away to smile faintly at Aidan. "A hunter came and saved the day."

Aidan smiled faintly back.

Angie faced Sebastian again, only to catch him giving Aidan a quick look of surprise. She was curious enough to wonder about the look but not curious enough to ask. The less she knew about Sebastian the better. She was already dreading the idea of saying goodbye for some reason, and she didn't like that she felt this way. Liked even less that she didn't fully understand her own reaction.

He met her gaze again. Her heart beat a little harder and her stomach danced a giddy jig.

Or maybe she did understand her reaction to him. Maybe that was the problem.

She didn't belong in the demon hunters' world. She was a college student who needed to study for her midterms. She was a practicing witch who still had plenty to learn. The magic was a constant discipline that took years of study and focus. It was her calling, her…identity. She was a witch.

And that meant getting to know a handsome demon hunter any better than she already did was dangerous.

The waitress came to clear their plates and ask if they wanted anything. Angie and Sebastian ordered tea. Aidan ordered another Coke. When the tea arrived, Sebastian scowled at the tea bag next to his mostly warm cup of water.

"Something wrong?" she asked him.

"This isn't tea." He held up the little bag and shook his head. "This is an abomination against tea."

She pressed her lips together, trying not to laugh. "So you're a tea snob, then."

"Not a snob. I just have functioning taste buds."

She chuckled at the face he made as he dunked the bag in his tepid water.

Yeah. Definitely dangerous getting to know him any better.

To her relief, they stopped talking about demons as they finished their drinks. They talked about nonsense like the best teas, and a good place in the US to get actual proper tea —what Sebastian considered proper tea—and no one asked any more questions about how she broke through the barrier between demon realms and this one just by looking through a tree.

The truth was, she didn't know herself. No one had been able to explain the *how* to her. Aidan hadn't had any answers. Neither had her mentor Esmerelda. Though Esmerelda had given her the pentagram charm to help her stay in control in the moments when she opened that barrier.

But in her studies, she had, occasionally, tried to look up the origin of her skill. Any information about what it was, how it had happened, how she could better control it.

Could she get rid of it?

And she'd come up with so little as to make the information useless. Not even a mention of how it was possible. No Druid curses that she could find. No warnings. No advice. It was something she did and she had no way to explain how it worked. If she stared between the V in a tree trunk, the layer between realms thinned. Dragging her gaze away from that opening could sometimes be difficult, feel almost impossible. And sometimes, something surprising and small was all it took to divert her attention. Breaking the contact was both physically difficult when she tried to force her gaze away, and breath-stealingly easy when something startled her out of her stare.

She didn't have an explanation for any of it. Which bothered her sometimes. But mostly she tried not to think about it, and she just avoided looking into the natural V in tree trunks. That was discipline enough.

Only Aidan, Esmerelda, and her immediate family even knew she could do this. And now Sebastian. This wasn't something she discussed with anyone. Not even her witch teachers after Esmerelda. No one. She didn't discuss it with the people who did know either. For the most part, Angie had spent her life trying to manage this cursed-skill without actually acknowledging it existed.

And after tonight, she intended to continue doing that. After tonight, she was finished with doing demon things.

But as they stood to leave, as they walked toward the front door, Sebastian set a hand to the middle of her back as a slight guide around a weirdly placed table, and Angie's insides clenched and melted at the same time. A reaction that made her knees a little shaky. She sucked in a breath at the heat crawling through her from just his hand against her back.

He must have felt something too, or just noticed her reaction, because he didn't quickly drop the touch, letting his hand linger against her for a moment longer than was necessary. When he finally let his hand drop, she could practically feel the hesitance.

Or maybe that was her own hesitance and not wanting the contact to end.

She thanked the goddess she'd had her touch psychic skills well-controlled in that moment, as she always did inside places like restaurants with heavy traffic and a lot of things touched by other humans. She wasn't sure she'd be able to take any flashes of insight into Sebastian just then.

The hunters walked her to her hand-me-down Dodge in the small diner parking lot. "Thanks for everything tonight," Aidan said.

"Will they cause more trouble? The men from the cult?"

Aidan shrugged. "We'll take care of them. It's our job."

Not her job. Their job. She was a visitor to their world. Only a visitor.

A good reminder. For all of them.

She met Sebastian's gaze in a stare that lasted a moment too long, then hastily retreated into her car.

As she drove out of the parking lot, she glanced in the review mirror. Aidan had turned toward their rental car, but Sebastian was still staring after her as she left. She raised her hand a little, a goodbye gesture she wasn't sure he'd see. But he lifted his own hand, returning the gesture.

She fought her smile all the way home.

The night could have been a lot worse.

KAT SIMONS

Moonlit Strange

Moonlit Strange

CHAPTER ONE

*A*ngie Jordan let out a slow breath and tried not to breathe back in too deeply. She still gagged. The smell of sulfur and roasting meat coated the back of her tongue with rotten egg flavor, overcoming the more pleasant scents of damp earth, juniper, pine, and oak trees. After two years of doing this, she'd have thought she'd be used to the stench. But no. It still turned her stomach every time.

The ground beneath her was cold and hard, the damp soil leeching through her jeans. There'd be snow in this part of the Sandia Mountains soon. She could practically taste it. Or at least she had before the sulfur stink permeated all her senses. She welcomed the cold. It was a much-needed counterpoint to the heat from the escaped demon standing twenty feet below them.

She wasn't sure how she felt about a demon being loose practically in her backyard—well, at least the mountains east of where she lived in Albuquerque—but it did make returning home later easier than their usual hunts.

Around her, darkness had settled over the woods, which only made the demon's glow seem more intense, a strange sort of moon in the middle of the trees. Beyond the beast's glow, a pinpoint of light from a campfire, just visible in the distance, looking incredibly small and vulnerable.

The area was mostly quiet, all the wildlife vanished ahead of the demon's approach, so that when the demon chuckled quietly, the sound vibrated across her nerves in a sharp sting.

Crouched on the ground next to her, Sebastian leaned in close and whispered, "Almost ready?"

"I found the right tree," she murmured back in his ear so they wouldn't be overheard. His delicious scent helped push out the demon's rotten egg stench so she leaned in closer to him, breathing him in. "I'll be ready when you are."

She shivered at the brush of his lips against her cheek, and her heart pounded a little harder.

Below their vantage on a small ridge overlooking an oak and pine encircled clearing, the beast's red and yellow glow intensified, the lava that made up its skin starting to swirl. It had spotted its prey.

The creature hadn't even pretended to be anything but a demon. Most freed demons shapeshifted to the form of a human, or took over the body of a human, depending on the species. This one, newly freed and still stinking of its own realm, hadn't bother. It stalked through the trees in its melting lava form, shaped roughly like a human but with giant, curved horns on its head, hooves for its feet, and towering over an average human at nearly ten feet tall. Its eyes were a black so dark they looked like bottomless holes in its otherwise glowing face. And its mouth was filled with sharp sharp teeth.

The Fire Beast was such a classic, stereotypical image of a demon, she almost understood why it didn't try to hide its natural form. Watching that creature approach would send any human into a screaming state of terror, a flavor all demons savored.

And it was hers and Sebastian's job to banish the beast back to a demon realm so it couldn't kill again.

"I'll get between it and the campsite," he murmured, his English accent harder to detect when he whispered. "Will that give you enough room to work?"

She nodded. "That tree?" She pointed to the left and a few feet in front of the demon without actually looking at the tree in question. "That's the one. Aim for that."

"Stay safe," he said and this time kissed her on the mouth.

When he leaned away, she took one last moment to study his gorgeous face, his dark eyes bright in the demon's strange glow, the hint of red in their depths stronger as the fight approached. A trickle of sweat rolled down his dark temple, and she wondered at him allowing that. He was a hunter. He could will himself not to sweat.

She touched his cheek. He needed a shave.

"Stay safe, too," she murmured.

He winked and eased back, his movements surprisingly quiet for such a large man. But he was a demon hunter, with the will to fend off creatures most humans only thought about in nightmares. When you could will your blood to flow like molasses through your veins and will your own heartbeat down to almost nothing, moving quietly over the uneven ground, avoiding branches and dried leaves, was simple.

She fingered the pentagram charm on her bracelet, letting the familiar pattern press into her fingers even as her adrenaline surged.

She waited to move until Sebastian stepped from the darkness into the demon's path. The lava glow from the beast washed across Sebastian's dark skin, the weird illumination like red moonlight, a color that intensified the red tint in Sebastian's eyes.

A piercing burst of drunken human laughter filtered through the clearing from the distant campsite.

The beast chuckled, low enough to make the ground shiver. "You cannot stop me, tiny hunter," it said to Sebastian. "I am all powerful."

Angie picked that moment to scramble back down the hill, making her way to the tree she'd pointed out to Sebastian. She kept the two in sight, as much as she could, while creeping inside the treeline. Staring at them meant she would know in an instant if Sebastian was in trouble, but it also kept her from inadvertently looking at any of the surrounding trees before she was ready.

"Demons always say shit like that," Sebastian said, his accent rolling the words with a hint of Manchester. "And it's always a bluff." He pulled a large wooden cross from the thigh pocket of his canvas pants and held it in front of the beast. "Now it's time for you to return to where you came from."

"You think that symbol will work on me?" The demon sounded amused, but it took a step away from Sebastian.

Sebastian smiled. "You escaped a man who used this religion's symbols to call you. That makes you vulnerable to the symbols." He moved a few feet closer to the demon.

The Fire Beast straightened to its full height and held its position until Sebastian was within reach, then it snarled and stepped back another few steps.

"That won't banish me," the demon hissed. "I am free. I will feed and stay free in this realm filled with so much easy prey." A long tail, tipped with a wicked looking spike, unfurled behind the demon, and black wings that hadn't been there earlier rose above the beast's shoulders. "You can't stop me, little hunter."

"We'll see," Sebastian said.

Angie reached the tree she'd been aiming for but continued to keep her gaze on the demon and the hunter. She had to time this just right, or the beast might escape.

She'd already enclosed the distant human campsite in a protective circle, and because the campers were a little drunk, they'd thought having a real-life witch creating a magic circle around them was funny. They didn't believe an actual demon was approaching, but they were game for a party. Angie had promised to tell them their futures if they stayed put—and as a touch psychic, she was good at reading people and telling them what they wanted to hear, even if she didn't always get a look at their future when she touched them. So long as the group of humans remained around that campfire, inside the circle she'd drawn around them, they'd be safe.

The problems started when the demons got near enough for humans to see them. Then the humans tried to run away. Always. Running, breaking open the circle, left them vulnerable. And complicated her and Sebastian's task.

After the second time that had happened, she'd suggested they try to banish the demon before it reached the humans it was stalking. Too logical in hindsight.

The Fire Beast made a lunge toward Sebastian, but Sebastian held his ground and raised the wooden cross. The demon's skin flared a bright orange as it came up against the symbol and it hissed, lurching backward.

The power wasn't necessarily in the cross, though because a cross and various Christian symbols had been used to call this demon, those symbols worked against it. The real power, though, was in the will of the hunter.

A demon hunter had to have a will stronger than a demon's. If the hunter's will to triumph faltered, even a little, the beast would win and the hunter would die. Most of the time, the hunters tried to contain demons before they escaped the hold of the human who'd summoned them. Sometimes, they succeeded.

Sometimes, they arrived too late.

Once a demon was freed from the confines of whatever ceremony the summoner had used, it could do as it pleased in this realm. Breaking free cost a demon power, though. They couldn't cut themselves off from their own realm without losing something. The amount of power they sacrificed depended on the demon, the deal they'd made with their summoner, and the way they manipulated a break in that deal. The more powerful the demon, the more they lost to stay here. Most demons who made this move, however, didn't care.

Some hid in human form and just went about their business, escaping here to get away from stronger beasts, to avoid being prey themselves. The hunters usually left those creatures alone. So long as they didn't kill anyone.

Other demons escaped into this realm with the intention of causing destruction and chaos. Those were the ones the hunters went after.

This Fire Beast had eaten the human who'd called it, leaving behind a bloody stump of leg and a few fingers, the only evidence of the human. The authorities would attribute the murder to a human killer, someone crazy and dangerous. Days would be spent searching for the murderer, all to no avail.

It was better the population as a whole didn't really believe in demons. More might be called into this too-vulnerable realm if they did.

"I will not be sent back," the Fire Beast snarled at Sebastian and lunged for him again. The claws tipping the beast's hands glowed a fierce white.

Sebastian's eyes narrowed against the heat, but he didn't move and he didn't look away from the demon's gaze even as its claws swiped dangerously close to his ear.

Angie sucked in her gasp, holding her warning inside. She'd distract Sebastian if she yelled now. They'd done this enough, she'd learned to keep quiet until just the right time. Still, it never stopped terrifying her when the demons got that close to him.

"I will not be sent back," the beast roared.

And from the rolling lava of his body, it pulled out a fire sword, the blade made of the same glowing red lava as the monster. The sword was huge, easily six feet long, almost Sebastian's full height. When the demon swung the blade through the air, it made a whooshing noise and flames of light followed in its wake.

Sebastian tilted his head to one side as he studied the sword. "Pretty," he said.

The demon raised the blade high over its head and swung down, the tip of the blade aiming straight for the top of Sebastian's head.

CHAPTER TWO

Sebastian dove to one side, and the demon's sword bury deep into the earth where he'd just been. Angie couldn't help her gasp that time.

The ground sizzled. The smell of burning leaves and pine needles rose into the air, dampening the demon's sulfur stench. A small fire started near the sword, a fire that would turn into a raging forest fire if they weren't careful.

She cursed under her breath. She hated Fire Beasts.

The demon pulled its sword free of the ground and swung it at Sebastian again. Sebastian dove away, then raised the cross. The demon snarled and stumbled back a step. The tip of its sword touched the ground again, sparking another small fire. The demon flicked its tail over the flames, scattering the little sparks to make more little fires. Then it fanned its wings, adding oxygen to the mix.

Damn it.

Narrowing her eyes to focus her concentration away from Sebastian's fight, she breathed out the words of a rain spell, moving her hands in a long-practiced pattern, careful of her finger movements as she chanted. Pulling up her inner magic to aid the construction of the spell, she called on the element of water, focused on drawing the surrounding moisture to a single spot over their heads.

Careful. Careful.

Too much rain and the area would get treacherously slippery. Too little and the forest would burn.

She sensed, rather than saw, the gathering cloud, the pull of precipitation from the air into a concentrated ball, building and building, until with the final word of her spell, the last, long drawn out word of the chant, and a flick of her fingers, the cloud burst and rained poured down over the clearing.

The fires the demon had started smoked and died. The demon's blade dimmed under the wash of water, its outer surface hardening into a black rock. Angie didn't have any illusions that would keep the sword from bursting into flames again, but it was a nice bonus. There wasn't enough water in the area to solidify the demon's body. That would take a storm so big it would be as dangerous as the beast itself. But containing its sword, even for a few minutes would help Sebastian.

And the damage to its sword distracted the demon. It roared and shook the weapon, then bashed it against a nearby tree. The tree cracked, toppling backward in a loud crash of breaking branches and splintering wood.

Angie winced. That tree had fallen away from them, but

if the demon decided to, it could flatten the whole area, dropping trees onto their heads. Sebastian might be able to will the trees from falling on him, but she didn't have a handy magical shield that could take that kind of weight.

They had to get the beast back to its realm. Now.

The demon laughed and swung its still hardened sword at Sebastian. Sebastian rolled under the swing, coming up closer to the demon instead of moving farther away from it. He raised his wooden cross, and the demon covered its eyes with its free hand even as its skin brightened orange again.

Sebastian pulled off the base of the cross, revealing a long, thin, sharp knife. He sliced it across the demon's exposed chest and then rolled away from the beast's wild swing, coming up in a crouch a few feet away.

Angie took that as her moment. She braced herself, because this was always the hardest part.

For her.

This next step didn't take magic—in fact, she used the protection spell on the pentagram charm on her bracelet to help her *not* do this too often. It required something other than magic, a dangerous, exceedingly rare—thank the universe!—trait.

And through some very very bad luck, she'd been born with that trait.

She turned to the tree she'd located earlier, the one with its trunk forming a natural V-shape. Not Vs in the branches. Not some pieces broken off to cause that shape. The trunk of the tree had to split and grow out in two directions. She stared into the center of that V...

Seeing the demon realm through it without any effort at all.

Even at a glance, that world was there. Watching the fight between Sebastian and the Fire Beast, she'd been aware of the hellscape realm just at the periphery of her vision.

Now that she looked, now that she *saw* it, the smells leaked out. The heat. Just around the edges of the tree, she was still aware of the woods, the trees stretching out beyond the one she stared into, unaffected by what she witnessed. The barrier between realms softened. She could feel it getting thinner, weaker. And soon, if she wasn't very careful, something on the other side of that breach would notice.

If they spotted the opening, they'd take it. Spilling into this realm like a plague.

That had happened only once, but it was enough to haunt her nightmares to this day.

She fingered her pentagram, taking what strength she could from the charm, and called out, "Sebastian, now!"

Even to her own ears, her voice sounded deep and loud and not quite her own.

She couldn't turn away from the breach without closing it. As soon as her attention moved off the tree, the barrier between realms would thicken again. The weakness in the barrier would still be there, for her to open again if she *looked*, but nothing the other side would notice or could get through. They couldn't see the doorway between realms from that side, if she wasn't holding it open. She wouldn't have been able to either. There were no trees in this particular demon realm. Just heat and lava and sulfur and smoke. Blackness underfoot. An orange and red sky of fire overhead.

A hellscape worthy of the name.

Sounds from Sebastian and the demon's fight grew louder, and she knew Sebastian was driving the demon this way. She stood to the side but couldn't move too far from the tree or she wouldn't be able to hold open the breach. Still, she hoped there was enough room. Her job, right now, was to hold the rip between the realms open, to concentrate on that and that alone, until she saw the demon fall through.

Then she could look away.

Or at least try to.

Crashing. Curses. The demon's hiss. Another roar of anger. She winced when she heard another tree break and collapse, praying to the Goddess no trees collapsed on her. Praying the demon wouldn't figure out the one way to close the doorway between realms would be to hack off one arm of the tree trunk's natural V. Without that, she didn't see the demon realm beyond. It was out of her reach.

Under different circumstances, she was good with that.

Another distant sound reached her. More hissing. And chittering. Loud and insistent.

Not the chittering.

Not that.

Her heart hammered. The chittering meant more demons were approaching from the other side. Her ears hurt with the sound. Her nerves erupted in pain. Her teeth ached.

She couldn't see them yet, but oh how she hated that sound.

The sounds of the fight behind her got closer, but the tug and hold of the demon realm had her in its grip now. She stared into the hellscape and waited to see the demon fly through.

"No!" The demon's voice, loud above even the sounds of other approaching monsters. "I won't go back!"

"Be gone, demon." Sebastian's voice, deep and powerful. Cutting through the noise in her head. "You will not run free in my realm." His command carried power. Not the power of the symbol in his hand, the knife it had hidden…

This was the power of his will.

Even Angie felt that power, rolling over her. Compelling the demon forward. That strength of will never cease to amaze her. And Sebastian's power gave her the will to hold her place. Not to flinch when she felt the demon's heat on her right. Not to turn away and lose the connection to the demon realm.

From the corner of her eyes, she saw the glow of the monster, bright now, and very orange under Sebastian's assault. It hacked downward with its sword.

Temptation to check on Sebastian. She ignored it.

More of the demon pushed into her view. One arm raised to ward off Sebastian, the other holding the sword up over its head like a knife, stabbing downward again and again.

Sebastian's voice. "You will not run free in my realm. Be gone, demon." He rolled the words with so much power, the demon stumbled back another few inches closer to the breach.

"Be gone," Sebastian said, louder. Then again, even louder.

The hairs on Angie's arms rose. A chill rushed through her body. She didn't turn away from the hellscape.

The demon roared a denial. Tried to push forward. But the realm had him now. The other side dragged him back, like calling to like, nature righting itself by returning things to where they belonged. Between the call of its own realm, and Sebastian's will to win this fight, the demon didn't stand a chance.

It screamed another denial and threw its sword at Sebastian. She didn't see where it landed, but Sebastian's voice assured her he was still safe.

The beast grabbed at the tree trunk as its realm sucked it in. It used its wings to try and block the doorway. The tree trembled but wouldn't break now. The demon was caught. Stuck inside the opening of its realm and holding it open, even without Angie's abilities.

The fact that the opening couldn't close while the demon resisted its pull wasn't good.

Sebastian stepped into her peripheral view now. "You've lost," he said, his voice still deep and powerful, but quieter now. "Be gone, beast. This is not your time."

"I will not lose," the demon hissed. "I have earned this right to feed."

"No." Sebastian said simply. "No."

The hairs on the back of Angie's neck rose as Sebastian's will washed over and past her. She only felt it this powerfully, so distinctly, in these fights. He used it in other circumstances, but this was when she really *felt* it.

And it was strong.

The demon's wings bent and tore along the thick, black membrane as it was pushed back into its realm by Sebastian's will. It roared another denial. But too late…

It collapsed backward into the hellscape with a sucking, popping sound that made Angie gag.

"Now," Sebastian murmured.

She started to turn away.

A strange voice from behind them said, "Dude, how drunk am I?"

Sebastian turned toward the human with bad timing.

And a long, spike-tipped tail flicked out through the still open breach between realms and wrapped around Angie's ankle.

Pulling her through the V in the tree trunk…

Into the demon realm.

CHAPTER THREE

ngie screamed. She was too surprised to do anything else. She heard Sebastian call her name, but she couldn't focus on that.

Because she was in the demon realm.

Where there were no trees.

She was no longer holding open the breach between realms. It was about to collapse.

The chittering noise of approaching demons got louder.

Panic and horror made her pulse rush so fast, the sound almost overwhelmed the nails-on-a-chalkboard sound of the approaching horde. She could still feel the opening, still see through to the woods beyond, but that opening was starting to shrink.

The Fire Beast laughed behind her. "If I must be here, human, I will have a final snack."

It still had its tail wrapped around her ankle, and it started dragging her along the burning rocks. Slowly. To increase her terror.

She kept her gaze on the breach, terrified if she looked away she'd lose it, even though there wasn't a tree here for her to look through. She wasn't thinking with any kind of logic, just pure animal panic and terror.

Feeding the approaching demons.

She scrambled against the hard, black surface, her skin burning, her nails breaking against rocks that stabbed with sharp edges like glass. She had just enough sense left, around the panic, to summon a spark spell. It wasn't a dramatic spell, but it was one she'd used enough on her brothers as a kid, it was instinctive and ingrained. She didn't have to think about the words, or the twist and flick of her fingers to seal the spell.

A spark of electricity, sharp and powerful, traveled down her leg and buzzed with enough voltage into the demon's tail, the beast snarled and leapt away.

Freeing her ankle.

She scrambled on hands and knees toward the slowly closing doorway. How was it still open? Terror closed her throat. Panic had tears running down her cheeks. She lurched awkwardly, too afraid to even get back to her feet.

The sound of approaching demons, the hiss of the Fire Beast, the sizzle of her skin on the hot rocks, the smell of sulfur and burnt meat…her burning clothes…her skin…

She threw herself at the breach as the demon's tail cracked out again, a whip wrapping around her ankle. She hissed the spark spell again, giving it enough magic to sting her even as it jolted the demon backward. She couldn't think to form another spell, but her fear fed the spark spell, making it more intense and stronger than she normally allowed. She poured power into the electrical jolt because it was all she had.

The chittering grew louder, so loud now, she couldn't hear the Fire Beast over it. The heat of their approach choked her, stealing what breath she had left.

They were coming.

They were here.

And the breach was almost closed.

She'd be trapped. She was too far away to reach the opening. The demons were almost on her.

She repeated the spark spell, over and over, powering it with magic she pulled from her very core, creating a halo of electricity around her that sent anything that got close enough to touch flying backward. On hands and knees, still muttering the spell, her gaze still locked with the shrinking doorway, she made one final lunge.

"Angie!"

A familiar hand reached through the opening, dark and strong, reaching for her.

She lurched up and grabbed Sebastian's wrist as he wrapped his fingers around hers, locking her in his hold. The electricity around her leapt over his skin in blue sparks of light, but the shock of it didn't seem to affect him.

Or his hold on her.

So strong and solid it was like fresh air against her burning skin. She clung to him as the scrambling behind her intensified, the sounds of the demons drowning out all other noise. Except the sound of her thumping heart.

She looked up into Sebastian's face, the intensity of his stare, gripped his arm with her other hand to hold tighter. And with a mighty effort…

He pulled her through the vanishing doorway.

They landed in a heap on the other side, her on top of Sebastian as he collapsed back into the dried leaves and pine needles covering the forest floor. Cool air, the smell of damp, cold earth. Sebastian's warm body under hers.

Angie felt the opening between realms snap shut, heard the cacophony of angry denials and protests from the demons as the barrier solidified, sealing them off from her world. She didn't dare look over her shoulder at the tree.

She buried her face against Sebastian's neck, her heart hammering hard enough she was sure he could feel it. Sobbing breaths weren't enough to pull in oxygen and she started to see spots.

A gentle hand caressed down her spine. "Breathe, love. Breathe. I've got you. I've got you."

She let his words flow into her, beyond her logic and right to her primitive, terrified core. Letting the litany soothe that part of her that was too scared to even allow thought.

Eventually, her heartbeat slowed to a less terrifying speed. The spots cleared from her vision. She hugged him close, the residual terror of what had just happened leaving her weak.

"I've got you," he murmured into her hair.

"Thank you for reaching for me," she whispered back.

"Always."

The sounds of the hellscape had vanished, though the glare and burn of it still crowded her vision when she closed her eyes. As her fear eased, the pain set in, and she realized she had burns, cuts and scrapes, maybe even a sprained ankle to deal with.

None of it seemed particularly urgent just then.

From a few feet away, someone said, "Dude, that was a trip."

She blinked and frowned up at the man standing at the edge of the clearing, still staring at the tree behind her. He was one of the campers, a thin young man bulked up by a heavy coat and a wool beanie pulled down over his shaggy brown hair.

He shook his head, his eyes wide. "I need to give up the drink, dudes."

Angie closed her eyes and started to laugh.

CHAPTER FOUR

She woke screaming. The heat, the sting of glass-sharp rocks tearing her skin, the sound of chittering demons followed her out of the dream.

Strong arms came around her, holding her tight. And reality settled as Angie breathed him in, clearing the memory of sulfur from her nose, took in her surroundings. She burrowed against Sebastian, her fingers going to the pentagram charm hanging from her bracelet. She rubbed the small silver medallion until she could no longer hear the demons right next to her ear.

"Another one, eh?" he whispered after a time.

"They aren't getting any better." She swallowed hard, finally leaning away from him to get the glass of water she'd left on the nightstand, ignoring the mostly empty bottle of Tequila next to it. Though she was sorely tempted. She gulped down the water, letting the cold sooth her raw throat. Raw from the scream or the memory of pain, she wasn't sure.

"It'll take time, love," Sebastian said, sitting up in bed and letting the sheets fall down around his hips.

He was shirtless, all heat and muscle and strength, a faint glow lighting his dark skin from the moonlight streaming in through the open curtains. And she wanted so badly to just collapse back into his arms and pretend nothing was wrong.

But everything was wrong.

Most of her injuries had healed. The worst of the burns were now just red lumps of healing skin. She could put weight on her ankle again.

But the psychological damage of nearly being trapped in a demon realm…

That hadn't lessened even a little bit.

The panic attacks, the nightmares, the terror of what *might* have happened were almost worse than the actual horror in the moment. Imagining what could have been—the torture, the pain—even now that she was fully awake, those thoughts left her pulse racing and another panic attack just at the edge of her awareness, waiting to strike.

She rolled out of bed instead of rolling into Sebastian, avoiding his arms when he reached for her. She shivered now that she wasn't enveloped in their warm bed, under warm blankets. She snatched her terrycloth robe off a nearby chair and wrapped herself up in it, trying to keep the cold from settling into her bones.

It didn't feel any better than the sizzling heat from her nightmare had felt.

She curled herself up into the chair that had held her robe and set her chin on her knees as she stared across the space at Sebastian. Holding his gaze was hard. She didn't want to do this. She'd been thinking it for weeks and avoiding the decision. Her heart broke and her throat clogged up on the words.

But things weren't getting any better. And they wouldn't as long as nothing changed.

Oh but the pain of what she had to do… Damn the demons anyway. Damn them for giving her this and then forcing her to leave it.

She said the words that ripped her world into tiny pieces. "This isn't going to work."

He nodded, but his eyes narrowed. "You can't come with me on hunts anymore."

She wanted to cry. "More than that. I can't… I can't have anything to do with the demon world anymore." When he didn't respond, she forced herself to say the thing she didn't want to say aloud. "Anything. I can't…" She swallowed hard and rushed on, her words spilling out. "We can't be together anymore. I'm going to move."

"Albuquerque's your home. Your family's here. Where will you go?"

She didn't miss that he skimmed over the part where she said they had to separate. Was he accepting or avoiding? "I have a friend in New York. She works at a place where I can get a job pretty easily."

"Reading cards and telling people what they want to hear," he snapped.

And there it was. The pain and anger. She supposed that was better than indifference. "Yes," she said. "I'm good at reading people and helping them."

"Then go be a counselor," he said. "You're better than some sideshow freak reading fortunes."

"You know that's not what I do," she said, her voice dull. She couldn't even get angry and fight back. She didn't have the heart for it.

She'd just shattered her heart.

He threw off the blankets and stood, pacing through their bedroom in his boxer shorts, his muscles flexing as he moved, his jaw tight under his night stubble. No gray in the black, not yet. Maybe not ever if he didn't want it. A silly thought at such a time. She was working overtime to distract herself.

"You don't have to do this," he said, facing her, hands on his hips, the moonlight at his back. "Not go this far. You know you don't."

"Sebastian…" She looked away because looking at him hurt too much. "I love you. But your life, everything you are is wrapped up in being a demon hunter. You go where you're needed. And you are needed. I can't stand in the way of that." She met his gaze long enough to say, "And you can't walk away from it either."

Which was true. Demon hunters didn't quit. They wouldn't *be* hunters if they weren't strong enough for the job, at least not for long. Hunters who weren't strong enough died. No one quit. No one retired. She wasn't even sure they could. The urge to go where a demon was overwhelmed

Sebastian when it came on him. And he went. Almost like a trance, except he was aware of what he was doing. The instincts took over. He could no more end those instincts than he could stop the blood flowing through his veins.

She almost laughed—a nervous, mildly hysterical reaction—when she realized that because of his will, he actually could stop his own blood flow if necessary, or at least slow it substantially. But he couldn't ignore the call of the hunt.

She could tell by the way his shoulders drooped he knew she was right about that last at least. "You will continue to hunt," she said. "As is right. You're good at it, and I'm not asking you to try giving it up. That wouldn't be good for anyone. But this world of yours… I don't belong in it."

"You were made for it or you wouldn't be able to do what you do," he said, his voice quiet, deeper with his emotions.

"If I were made to be a hunter, I would be one. I'm not. I don't have the will for it. I'm a witch. I'm called to that life. My powers, my strengths bend that way." She shook her head. "And I can't keep pretending I'm able for this path, just because I don't want to give you up."

"You're upset because of what happened. It's still raw. Give it time."

"That's what I'm doing. Time. Maybe even some counseling of my own." Though what the hell counselor she'd be able to talk to about nearly getting stuck in a demon world… She supposed there had to be someone in the magical community who could help.

"Ending our relationship isn't necessary," he said.

"Moving across the country isn't necessary. You can recover here. I can help. When I'm not hunting, I can be here for you."

"And every time I look into your eyes, into eyes I love, I will see that red deep in the depths of the brown. And I'll remember all of it. I can't get past it when I'm continuing to look into it every day."

His jaw so tight she thought he might break a tooth, he spun away from her, cursing under his breath. He ran his hands over his head, over his short, tightly trimmed dark curls. Then made fists against the back of his neck.

She stayed where she was, watching him. Swallowing her desire to take back everything she'd just said and stay. She'd been swallowing this conversation for weeks. Hoping she'd get better. Hoping she'd find another solution.

She couldn't pretend anymore. Even as she watched him start to pace again, the nightmare images of the demon realm taunted her, her imagination calling up all the horrors that could have been. The only thing that had been good in that moment was seeing his hand thrust through the breach, reaching for her, pulling her out.

But what if he'd been a moment slower? What if she hadn't gotten to him in time? What if the demons had broken through her spark spell? She'd been surrounded. Terrified. Too panicked to recall any other defensive spells.

And the demons had been hungry.

She felt her panic rising again, sweeping through her in a blood pounding rush, and she had to put her head between her knees to keep from hyperventilating.

Damn it, damn it, damn it. Why? Why couldn't she control this so she could stay?

The soothing weight of his hand on her upper back only made things worse because his touch made her feel better. Tears leaked down her cheeks.

"I can't do this, Sebastian," she murmured as another sob took her. "I have to get some distance. I can't recover here. Like this." *With you.*

He pressed his lips to the back of her head, then set his cheek against her hair. "I can't let you go forever, Angie. I can't face that. I'd give up everything else first."

She raised her head to protest but he quieted her with a finger across her lips.

"But I will give you time and space. For now." He cupped her cheek. "When you've had time to recover, to get some perspective, we'll come back to this conversation."

"And what if I can't get past this? What if I can never come back?"

He held her gaze for a very long time. The moonlight played funny tricks, making the red glow in his eyes more obvious, giving the scene a strange sort of ambiance that only made her ache more.

"I can't consider that possibility," he murmured finally. "I don't want to. But I will deal with it if that's your decision. I just need you to keep open to the idea that this isn't the end for us."

She didn't want it to be the end either. She couldn't see a way around it, but she didn't want to think this was their last conversation, their last night together. So she nodded, and kissed him.

And in the morning, she packed a bag, got in her car, and drove to New York. Without looking back.

She didn't stop crying until she hit Ohio.

Thank you so much for reading this prequel duology to the Demon Witch series! I hope you enjoyed *Howling Dreadful* and *Moonlit Strange*! For the record, I did not realize how well the two titles would work together until well after I'd written and published the books. Only when I was putting this duology together and was trying to decide what to call it did I realize the two titles *fit*. So that was exciting.

These prequel stories aren't strictly necessary for enjoying the Demon Witch series, but I *love* reading all the little back story stories in big worlds, so I decided to write a couple, too. And writing these helped me get a handle on Angie's history with Sebastian and the demon world before the events of BONE LANTERN WITCH.

If this is the very first book you've read in the Demon Witch series, you probably love chronological order storytelling and I appreciate that. Next up, BONE

LANTERN WITCH, the first novel in the main series. And if you keep reading, you can read an excerpt!

This series arose from my curiosity about a secondary character in my Cary Redmond urban fantasy romance series. Angie started out as one of Cary's best friends. But she kept dropping hints about her life before Portland into Cary's stories and I knew I wanted to know more about all that. And the Demon Witch series was born.

Writing the series, when I knew where the main character would end up was an especially fun challenge! So if you want to see more of Angie and Sebastian (they do get a happily-ever-after, I promise. I did cut my teeth writing romance novels after all), don't miss the full Demon Witch series. And if that's not enough, be sure to check out the Cary Redmond series. You can start with *When Cary Met Angie* to see how the two future best friends first connect, then *Cary and the Demon Witch* for see some of Angie's past creep into her new life. Then start with THE TROUBLE WITH BLACK CATS AND DEMONS.

If you want to learn all there is to know about this big universe, or even my other fiction, the best places to do that are my store, my website, and my author newsletter. The store, KatSimonsBooks, and website, katsimons.com, both have up-to-date reading orders for series and are regularly updated with new release information and news. The store is a great place to see what's happening with my publishing, get exclusive stories and merch, and to support the author directly. Also, on the 1st and 15th of the month, I post a free-to-read short story in The Café at KatSimonsBooks. So lots of fun options for readers!

My author newsletter, which typically comes out monthly —unless there's something special going on—will also keep you updated on new releases as well as providing background news, looks ahead, occasional cover reveals, excerpts, coupons to my store, and occasionally full books for free. In fact, new subscribers get two exclusive-to-the-newsletter stories, one in my paranormal romance Tiger Shifters series and one in the Cary Redmond series.

If you prefer, you can also follow my author pages at BookBub, Facebook, or your favorite book vendor. And I do lurk on social media, mostly liking other people's posts, but I'm still there for a chat if you catch me! As I write this, I'm mostly on Bluesky and Instagram. You can also email me any time! I love hearing from readers.

Thanks again for reading *Howling Dreadful on a Moonlit Strange*!

~Kat

The Demon Witch

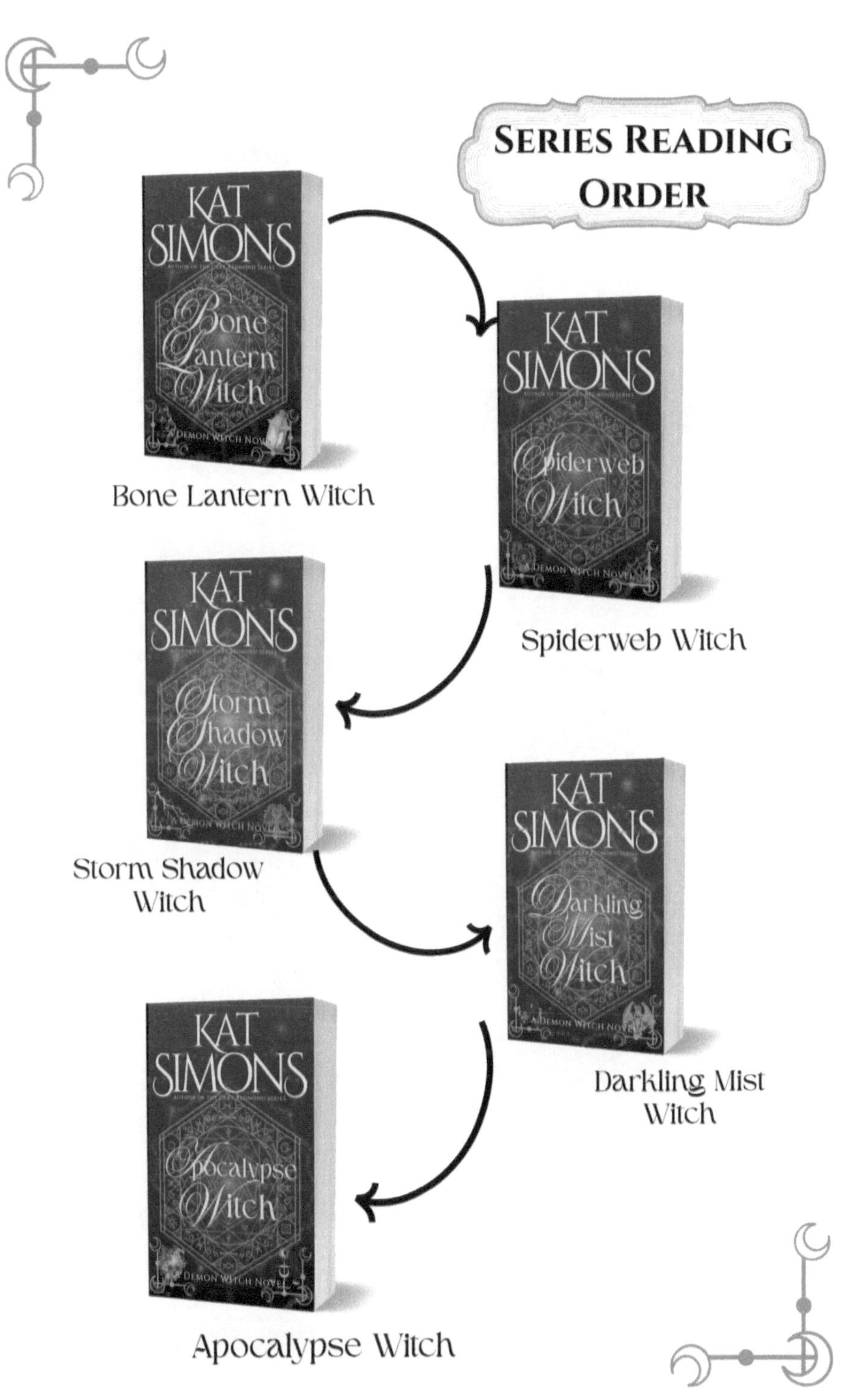

Bone Lantern Witch

Spiderweb Witch

Storm Shadow Witch

Darkling Mist Witch

Apocalypse Witch

KAT SIMONS

AUTHOR OF THE CARY REDMOND SERIES

Bone Lantern Witch

A DEMON WITCH NOVEL

BONE LANTERN WITCH

A DEMON WITCH NOVEL

EXCERPT

CHAPTER ONE

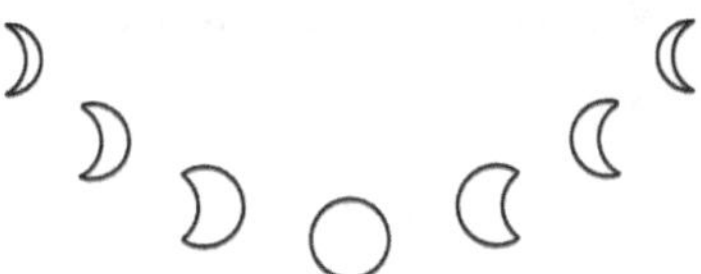

*A*ngela Jordan fingered her pentagram bracelet and stared at the natural V-shape formed by the split trunk of the small oak tree. She'd tried not to look, had managed to avoid looking on accident for years. But this tree sitting innocuously along the path from the Mosholu entrance in the New York Botanical Gardens had caught her off guard.

Or maybe her guard was down because of why she was here.

She rubbed the dangling silver pentagram charm in slow clockwise circles, pressing into the pattern with each pass over the top of the dime-sized disk. She took a step toward the tree. A slight tremor from the charm stopping her. The scent of sulfur and heat burned her nostrils, a sharp contrast with the cool autumn air. Ordinary, mundane humans walked behind her on the paved path, ignoring her, unable to see the horror she watched between the oak's trunk.

They were all so luckily innocent, she thought, as a demon from the hellscape noticed her.

She froze. Even her fingers stilled on the pentagram. Her heartbeat pounded. Panic she hadn't felt in months rushed through her blood stream.

If she could just stay still enough, maybe it wouldn't realize she could see it, maybe it wouldn't know.

The creature swiveled its head and flicked the air with its forked tongue, its red-eyed gaze narrowing. Its skin was the color of rolling volcanic lava, hard sections of black covered its chest and thighs, under that a luminous red and yellow glow. It hissed, though she couldn't hear the sound yet, revealing rows of shark-sharp teeth.

She tried to swallow without making any movements, not while it was looking at her. She failed.

The demon raced across the burning, charred land. Charging her. Barreling toward the rip she'd created between its realm and hers. It ran on all fours, even though it was vaguely human shaped, its spiked tail high behind it.

A lesser fire beast. Not the same species exactly. Not the same one as that night.

But the same hellscape.

The same realm.

She held her ground, unable to move even if she'd wanted to, glued by panic and fears she'd worked for almost two years to overcome. The stink of sulfur intensified, along with the burning smell of oak. Ash coated her tongue. An illusion she couldn't ignore.

The demon hit the tree and reached through the split in

the trunk, grasping hands tipped with impossibly long claws stretched toward her. She could hear its screams now, so high-pitched the sound ripped across her nerves, piercing and sharp. Its mouth stretched and distorted with its cries, taking shapes no being of this realm could manage.

Laughter and the chatter of a child moved behind her. The real world. Oblivious to the nightmare trying to reaching them. They'd see it if it got out, if any of the beasts escaped. The humans would see it.

And they'd know she let it free.

Angie folded her hand around her pentagram charm, encompassing the white beads of the bracelet itself where it hung loosely around her wrist. The charm burned coldly in her palm, the sensation a reassuring jolt of reality and sanity. A soft breeze moved through her hair, ruffling the baby hairs on her forehead, making her hanging moon earrings tinkle lightly.

Unless she was working, she didn't wear the stereotypical trappings of a psychic and witch. Not what mundane humans expected. No flowing skirts and excessive silver jewelry. No braids or patchouli-scented perfume. Today, she wore her comfortable camouflage—jeans and a t-shirt, hiking boots and a light autumn jacket. Only the pentagram bracelet, which she never risked taking off, and the earrings—a present from her brothers to represent her love of astronomy more than her witchy gifts—even hinted at her lineage.

None of it revealed her most horrible skill.

The sounds of the demon's screams got louder, a hissing and screeching that raised the hair on her arms. Behind it, more demons noticed the breach. Noticed her. They piled against the thin barrier, pushing through the V made by the oak's trunk like a writhing mass of snakes about to spill into this world.

A tug on Angie's jacket made her breath catch. She sucked in cool air, swallowed her screech, and glanced down.

A little girl, maybe five or six years old, looked up at her with wide eyes and a shy smile. Angie heard the screams of protest from the oak, the sounds piercing her skull. She smiled at the little girl in her unicorn t-shirt and pink ballerina skirt. The gold plastic crown tucked into her tightly curled black hair glittered in the autumn sunlight.

When the girl tugged Angie's jacket again, Angie bent lower so she was eye level with the child, moving her big purse to one side so it wouldn't get in the way.

"Are you a model?" the girl asked, her whisper not very quiet.

Angie chuckled. "No," she said. "Are you?"

The girl giggled and bounced on her toes. "I'm gonna be," she confided. "But right now I'm a princess."

"Yeah you are," Angie said. "And a beautiful one at that."

The girl's mother spotted the conversation and hurried over. "Sorry," she said. "I hope she wasn't bothering you. She's convinced you're a model."

"No problem." Angie waved to the girl as her mother pulled her up the paved road toward the children's section of the gardens.

The scent of sulfur had faded, leaving only the faint spoiled-egg taste of it in Angie's mouth.

She glanced at the oak from the corner of her eye, not making the same mistake she'd made earlier. She could still see the faint glow of the hellscape beyond, but the barrier between realms had solidified.

No demons would be climbing through today.

She pushed her hair out of her face, letting the breeze cool the sweat at her temples. When she felt settled, she tugged her jacket sleeves down, covering her bracelet, though she curled her fingers up into the sleeve to brush the charm one last time. She adjusted her purse at her hip, straightening the strap over her shoulder and across her chest.

Then, letting the fresh scents of green grass, damp earth, and the faint smell of hot sauce from the food truck at the front of the gardens clear out her senses, she moved on, studiously ignoring all the natural Vs formed in the trunks of trees.

Angie met him at the pavilion in the decorative conifers section of the gardens. Here, dozens of varieties of pines filled the rolling hills, scenting the air. Angie loved conifers. Very few of them grew with split trunks.

"How many times do I have to tell you I'm not doing this anymore," she said as she approached the loan man sitting inside the gray stone pavilion.

The open top let light spill across his face, making him look younger than his almost forty-three years. His short dark hair was still free of any hint of gray, his brown skin smooth, no creases or laugh lines around his dark brown eyes or full mouth. Sometime in the last year, he'd gone from clean shaven to a dark mustache and goatee-style beard, also without any gray.

Sebastian was a demon hunter, though, and they never looked their age. It wouldn't matter if he was forty-three or sixty-three or even eighty-three. Demon hunters remained exactly the age they wanted to stay. They willed away the process of aging the way they willed away demons called to this realm.

A demon hunter's will was an awesome thing to behold. A rare trait in humans, that kind of will. Rarer still that innate skill put to good use. And it was a trait fewer and fewer possessed with each passing year. Still, there were enough to keep the demon realms at bay. For now. It was their job to fight the fights and keep this world blissfully unaware of the threat.

At least, most people were blissfully unaware.

She refocused on Sebastian. He wore jeans and a burnt orange sweater that served to both honor the season and show off his broad shoulders and strong physique. The color suited him. Even without the softening glow of the afternoon sunlight, he would look good, though. A gorgeous, stunning man in his prime.

Her chest ached. She ignored it.

As she sat next to him, cradling her overlarge faux-leather purse in her lap, she reminded herself, again, demon hunting was his job. *Not* hers.

He studied her, his head tilted to one side as his gaze traveled over her face, lingering on her eyes, her lips. "You're looking good, Ang," he said, his voice deep, the English accent prominent.

She gestured at the surrounding trees, ignoring the compliment and the way his voice always sent a little tingle along her spine. "The Botanical Gardens was an interesting choice. Unless we're here for a specific reason. Either way, the answer is no."

He grinned, quick and sudden, an expression that gave him a boyish charm. That smile had always gotten her into trouble. "Maybe I just wanted to see you again," he said.

"If that were the case, we could have met for a coffee in a crowded café in the city. No reason to get me out here where no one will overhear our conversation."

"I could have kept anyone from overhearing our conversation even in a crowded café," he reminded her.

"We both know you didn't call me for a friendly reunion." Unfortunately. She swallowed that response. "Or anything else personal. We both know this is business."

In the first six months after they'd broken up, when she'd been determined to be done with demon hunting because it had nearly killed her, he'd come to her several times in New York, trying to coax her back into his world. She'd made the mistake of following him into two more hunts before she'd put her foot down for good. Two more hunts she should never have been involved in after...

She let out a long breath. "I'm not dealing in your business anymore. I can't do it again, Sebastian. I can't."

His smile dropped away. "I wouldn't ask if it wasn't

necessary. I don't like putting you through this any more than you like going through it."

She snorted. "Right. Which is why you keep dragging me back in."

She'd been trying to put the demon world behind her for almost two years. She'd worked hard to settle into a life without demons and hunters. Or at least, she'd tried to.

She hadn't seen Sebastian in a year and a half, after yet another hunt went horribly wrong for her. She'd finally, finally demanded he not contact her again unless it was an emergency. The last year and a half had been one of the most peaceful, uneventful times in her life. She'd loved it.

She wasn't going to give that up now, just because he flashed those gorgeous dark eyes at her. No matter how easy it was to ignore the hint of red in their depths. No matter how easy it was to fall back into the old ways, the old feelings.

"Ang," he said, drawing out her nickname. He held out his hand, palm up. "I tried to stay away. This time I really tried. But there's no one else like you in this world. And I need your help."

She let out a huff of a sigh and looked out over the trees, keeping her gaze on the solid trunk of a pine just down the hill from them. She'd known, when he texted her out of the blue, she'd known it would be something like this. Some demon related issue.

"No," she said without looking at him. She could still taste the sulfur and ash in her mouth from the earlier incident. That realm… The reminder helped her hold firm. "No, Seb. No more. Not ever again."

"I told her you wouldn't want to be involved," Sebastian said quietly. "I had to ask."

"Aidan?" Angie shook her head. "Of course."

Aidan was one of the oldest and most skilled demon hunters to walk this realm. No one was sure how old she was, or how long she'd been fighting demons. Just that she was still alive when so many others weren't. She was a legend among demon hunters. She was the hunter who'd found and trained Sebastian.

The hunter who'd rescued Angie from herself.

"You weren't her only option," Sebastian said. "Just a more straight-forward choice than any of the others left to us without you."

"I'm not going to ask," she said firmly, still not looking at him.

If she asked what the problem was, what they wanted her to do, she'd be halfway to giving in. She wouldn't be able to hear about the trouble and ignore it. He'd gotten her before with that trick. Better not to know. Better to stay ignorant and let the hunters handle it themselves.

"It's okay, Angie," he said, his voice quiet. "We'll save the child without you."

"You son of a bitch," she hissed. "Son of a bitch." She glared at him, her jaw tight. "I hate you for this."

He nodded. "I know."

"Bastard." She wrapped her fingers around the pentagram on her bracelet. "Tell me."

Bone Lantern Witch
Book 1 in the Demon Witch Series
Out Now!

BOOKS BY KAT SIMONS

Demon Witch Series

Howling Dreadful

Moonlit Strange

1-Bone Lantern Witch

2-Spiderweb Witch

3-Storm Shadow Witch

4-Darkling Mist Witch

5-Apocalypse Witch

Urban Fantasy

The Cary Redmond Series

Cary Redmond Short Stories and Collections

Joan of Kerry Series

Friday's Curious Shop Series

Paranormal Romance

Dragon Thief Series

Seven Families: Wolf Series

Tiger Shifters Series

Destiny Cats Series

Romancing the Leopard: A Tiger Shifters-Cary Redmond Crossover Novel

ALSO BY KAT SIMONS

Contemporary Fantasy

Haunts and Howls Collections

**Tombstone Wizard * The Unshattered Sword * Going Out of Business: Everything's for Sale * Anger Management * Demonic Dates * The Museum of Small Art's Everyman * Burning Inside a Stone Circle * Bored Questless * I Just Ate a Bug * Ting Ling * Sophie Saves the World * Black Water Hawthorns * To Dance in Fallow Fields at Midnight * The Troll and the Dressmaker*

Stories from the Café

The Café Collections

Stories from the Café: Volume One

Pick Your Genre Collections

Who Steals a Dragon

Contemporary Romances

Designed for You

Poinsettias and Possibilities

Mystery and Thriller

ROSS AND O'NEILL ADVENTURES

Galileo's Pendulum

ABOUT THE AUTHOR

Kat Simons earned her Ph.D. in animal behavior, working with animals as diverse as dolphins and deer. She brought her experience and knowledge of biology to her paranormal romance and urban fantasy fiction, where she delights in taking nature and turning it on its ear. She writes urban fantasy, contemporary fantasy, and paranormal romance in series which combine action adventure, the otherworldly, and a frequent dose of sexy romance.

The newest book in her bestselling romantic urban fantasy series about Protector Cary Redmond, The Trouble with Shifters and Fae Courts, sees a new direction for the intrepid Protector, her sexy leopard shifter mate, and the entire crew. Kat also launched a new novella length Urban Fantasy Romance series that follows the adventures of a magical thief and the dragon shifter prince she just can't seem to shake—and really doesn't want to. The first season of the Dragon Thief series released throughout 2024. Season Two begins in 2025 with The Crown of Kingship Job.

For something a little different, Kat also publishes fantasy, science fiction, and the occasional hockey romance under the name Isabo Kelly (https://www.isabokelly.com).

After traveling the world, living in places like Hawaii, Germany, and Ireland, Kat now lives in New York City with her family and a library's worth of books.

For more on Kat and her future books

Website: https://www.katsimons.com/
Newsletter: https://bit.ly/KatSimonsNewsletter

KatSimonsBooks

https://www.katsimonsbooks.com
https://www.TheCafeatKatSimonsBooks.com

Social Media

Facebook Page: https://www.facebook.com/
KatSimonsAuthor
BookBub: https://www.bookbub.com/authors/kat-simons
Bluesky: https://bsky.app/profile/katsimons.bsky.social
Instagram: https://www.instagram.com/isabokelly/
Threads: https://www.threads.net/@isabokelly

Join Kat's Newsletter

Stay Up-to-Date

On all Kat's News, Updates, and fun extras

New Subscriber Get Two Exclusive Stories Just for Signing up!

bit.ly/KatSimonsNewsletter

The CARY REDMOND Series

GOT TROUBLE?

Don't Miss a Single Book in this
Action-Packed Romantic Urban Fantasy Series